RIVER DANGER

RIVER DANGER

Thomas J. Dygard

MORROW JUNIOR BOOKS
New York

Copyright © 1998 by Thomas J. Dygard

Published by Morrow Junior Books
a division of William Morrow and Company, Inc.
1350 Avenue of the Americas, New York, NY 10019
www.williammorrow.com

Printed in the United States of America.

10 9 8 7 6 5 4 3 2 1

Library of Congress Cataloging-in-Publication Data
Dygard, Thomas J.
River danger/Thomas J. Dygard.
p. cm.
Summary: Although he reluctantly agrees to accompany his little
brother on a canoe trip, eighteen-year-old Eric finally gains new
respect for this younger sibling whose ingenuity rescues him.
ISBN 0-688-14852-2
[1. Brothers—Fiction.   2. Canoes and canoeing—Fiction.]   I. Title.
PZ7.D9893Ri 1998   [Fic]—dc21   97-36362   CIP   AC

This book is dedicated to
my son Tom, who was with me
on the Buffalo River and
some other rivers too.

CHAPTER 1

SITTING cross-legged on the rocky bar at the end of the road leading down to the river, Eric Douglas stared through gathering darkness at the rippling water. He barely noticed the old pickup truck pulling off the road and slowly moving across the bar, then coming to a halt at the water's edge. Eric glanced at it briefly and returned to his thoughts. Here he was, almost eighteen years old, just graduated from high school, and embarking on a canoe trip down the Buffalo River in the northern Arkansas Ozarks—with, of all people, his eleven-year-old brother, Robbie.

"What are those guys doing?" Robbie asked. He pointed at three men who had just gotten out of the pickup truck about thirty yards away.

Eric turned and squinted through the shadowy dusk.

Two of the men stood at the rear of the pickup, while the other climbed up into the bed. They unloaded a flat-bottom rowboat, then dragged it across the rocks and into the water.

That's weird, Eric thought. Who'd take a rowboat onto the Buffalo? Canoes, kayaks, and rafts were the usual—

"Hey, Eric, what're they doing?" Robbie asked again.

"Beats me," Eric said, then glanced back at his brother. "But don't stand there pointing at them. Sheesh, are you trying to make trouble for us?"

While one man held a rope attached to the boat, the other two walked back to the pickup truck, studying Eric and Robbie as they went. When Eric nodded a greeting, they didn't respond; they just turned away.

"Howdy to you too," Eric muttered to himself.

Eric and Robbie were the only other ones down by the river. In just a few weeks, the Buffalo would be swarming with hikers and canoers. Tents of varied colors and sizes would dot commercial campgrounds up and down the river. Children would be running all over the place, their parents calling for them to come back.

But now, in the middle of June, summer vacationers had not yet begun to arrive in masses, and Eric expected to see few others on the river.

In the growing darkness, lights were flickering on in the scattered houses of the nearby town of Gilbert. Tomorrow morning, Eric and Robbie would leave the town behind for the solitude of the woods and the river.

At the end of five or six days paddling down the Buffalo River, probably to the point where the Buffalo flowed into the White River, the two of them would hire a ride for themselves and their canoe back to Gilbert, load up the car, and drive home to St. Louis. Then Robbie would become the first Tenderfoot in his Boy Scout troop to win a Fifty-Miler Award—that is, if Eric could stand five or six days alone on the river and in a tent with him.

For sure, his kid brother was not his companion of choice for fifty miles of canoe camping on the Buffalo River.

As a matter of fact, Eric hadn't planned on taking any canoe trip at all during the two and a half months of summer leading up to the day he left for his freshman year at the University of Missouri.

It was true that he had loved canoe camping since the first time he and his father had shoved off from a rocky bank and begun paddling downstream. He loved everything about it—the rushing sound of small streams flowing over rocks, the smell of the woods, the fishing, the thrill of cooking the catch over a campfire, even the tough work of paddling the canoe, digging deep into the water with long strokes.

But none of that had been on Eric's schedule this summer. He was going to need spending money at the university, and his parents had made clear that it was up to him to provide it. So he had lined up five house-painting jobs and had planned to begin the first one on this very day.

But instead, here he was on the bank of the Buffalo River with Robbie.

Even with one week lost to paddling his brother down the Buffalo, Eric figured he could complete the five house-painting jobs before the end of summer, barring a lot of rain. So the loss of a week wasn't critical. Still, he had been eager to get going and not at all eager to share a canoe and a tent for a week with his younger brother.

Looking back, Eric knew he should have seen it coming from the day his father broke an ankle playing basketball at the YMCA.

For weeks before, his father and brother had planned their trip down the Buffalo, with Robbie's excitement level rising a notch with each discussion of the menu, each study of the map. Robbie had spent most of his life watching Eric and his father drive away with the canoe strapped to the top of the car, and listening afterward to their talk of the joys of the trip. Now, finally, he was going to have his turn. And, as a bonus, the new Boy Scout was going to win the Fifty-Miler Award for covering the distance in the wilderness.

Robbie did not seem to grasp immediately the significance of the white plaster cast on his father's ankle.

But Eric did. He knew that anybody with a cast on his ankle had no business canoeing through the wilderness. In the case of a spill—and anyone might spill—the cast would begin disintegrating. In the woods, that would be a disaster. Even without a spill, an emergency that required walking out of the woods would become not a chore but a calamity. And dragging the canoe over the gravel bottom of the shallows—and the Buffalo had some—would be impossible. No, the trip was off. Eric was sure of it. He was sorry for Robbie, but there was no other way.

Still, nobody said anything about canceling the trip for almost a week.

Then one night at dinner, John Douglas casually said, as if the thought had just occurred to him, "You know, I can't go canoeing with this cast on my ankle." He turned to Eric. "Why don't you go with Robbie instead?"

Eric gaped at his father. He opened his mouth, but no sound came out.

His father smiled, tilting his head a little as if to ask if Eric didn't agree it was a good idea. "It's only a week," he said. "You can spare the time. You'll still be able to get those houses painted. What do you say?"

Eric's eyes met his sister's across the table. Amy was fifteen, just out of the tenth grade. Her amused smile seemed to say, Gotcha, big brother. Eric did not smile back.

He glanced at his mother. She was waiting silently. Clearly, she had been in on the plot.

Robbie let out a whoop. "Yeah, man!" Maybe he had known that the cast on his father's ankle threatened his canoe trip. Maybe he had remained quiet, hoping his fears were ill-founded, or hoping something would happen to save the trip. And now something had.

Eric found his voice. "Me?" he managed. "Robbie? But he—"

"He's eleven years old—the same age you were when I took you on your first canoe camping trip. We not only survived but, as I recall, we had a pretty good time."

Eric swallowed. In a moment of silence, he decided against pleading that he needed to start painting. The argument didn't stand up. His father was right: He could spare a week. He knew he was trapped.

*　　*　　*

The two men were standing at the rear of the pickup truck, talking and looking across at Eric and Robbie.

Robbie, losing interest in the men, ran down to the river and began skipping flat rocks off the water.

Eric sat on the ground, arms hugging his knees, staring across the way, watching the two men out of the corner of his eye. He couldn't hear what they were saying, but from the frequent glances they were giving him, there was little doubt he and Robbie were the subject of their conversation.

One of the men turned and started walking toward Eric. He was wearing jeans without a belt, beat-up sneakers, a red T-shirt that had faded to pink, and a blue baseball cap. When he drew close, Eric noticed that he was a couple of days away from his last shave.

Eric managed a smile.

Robbie came running over to see what was happening. Maybe, for once, his brother would keep his mouth shut. Eric hoped so.

The man, still without offering a greeting of any sort, said, "Are you boys heading down the river this evening?"

"No," Eric said, getting to his feet. "We're staying here tonight." He gave a little nod in the direction of the campground up the road. "We're starting down in the morning."

The man stared at Eric for a moment. Then he nodded and, without saying another word, turned and walked back to the pickup truck.

"Not very friendly," Robbie said in an uncharacteristically low tone.

"No, not very."

After a moment of conversation, one of the men climbed into the bed of the truck and handed down a wooden box about the size of a laptop computer. The guy who took it stepped back and stumbled on a stone, nearly dropping the box. Eric could see the other two men cringe as the box almost fell, and the one who was still on the truck bed shouted, "Be careful, you moron! You could've blown us sky-high!"

Eric sat back down, positioning himself so that his back was mostly to the three men. He did not want to give the impression he was watching or that he was even interested in what they were doing. But out of the corner of his eye, he watched all three of them climb into the rowboat with the box and start to row upstream.

Robbie continued to stand and watch. "What are they doing?" he asked loudly.

"I'm not sure," Eric replied. "Come over here, and keep it down, will you?"

Robbie dropped to the ground next to Eric.

"Whatever they've got in that box is making them

pretty nervous," Eric said. "I've got a hunch it's dynamite."

"Dynamite," Robbie repeated, his eyes widening. "What for?"

"I bet they're planning to throw it in the river. Dad told me about it once. See, you toss a stick of dynamite in the water, and *blam!* It blows up underwater, and the shock waves scramble the fishes' brains for yards all around—knocks 'em out flat. The fish float up to the surface, and then all you have to do is scoop them in with a net. Totally illegal, of course, not to mention dangerous—you can blow yourself up along with the fish."

Robbie craned his neck to watch the men.

"How many times do I have to tell you?" Eric said impatiently. "Don't sit there gawking at them. They'll be gone in a minute."

Eric continued to watch out of the corner of his eye as the men rounded a bend upstream and disappeared.

"Shouldn't we call the police or a park ranger or something?" asked Robbie.

Eric gave a little wave toward the sky, now almost black, with stars beginning to appear. "Out here, call the police? And the rangers' station is miles downriver." Then he added, "Maybe it's not against the law—I don't know. Or maybe it is against the law but, well, sort of accepted around here. By the locals. Anyway—"

Just then, a deep, muffled booming, like a clap of far-off thunder, sounded from around the bend upstream, followed by barely audible hoots and shouts of laughter.

"I guess they got their fish," Eric said, shaking his head.

"I guess so," said Robbie. "Maybe we should go up to one of those houses and have them call—"

Eric sighed. He felt a little guilty about not trying to stop those men from dynamiting the river. But Robbie's pestering him about it was becoming annoying. "Look, it's late, and we're getting an early start tomorrow. At least I am. If you want to mess around all night trying to bust some guys for cheating a little—"

"Okay, okay," Robbie said.

Eric gave a last glance to the bend in the river upstream. He could still hear the men whooping and shouting, and then came another boom. Stupid jerks, Eric thought. But he was just one kid, and they were three grown men. What could he do?

"C'mon," Eric said to Robbie, getting to his feet. "Let's go fix supper."

CHAPTER 2

WHEN Eric came out of the tent in the morning, the sun was still low in the sky, a bright orange ball barely above the hills. There were no clouds in sight. The day was going to be hot, for sure. He made a mental note to make certain that Robbie kept his shirt on. Sunburn was bad in any case, but trying to paddle and drag a canoe with a blistered back was sheer torture. He and his friend Brent Crawford had learned the lesson the hard way during their first canoe trip together, when they had ignored one of John Douglas's strictest teachings.

Eric buckled his jeans, stretched his arms out wide, and then sat down. For a moment, he just stared through the haze. Then he picked up the old sneakers he wore for canoeing and began working his bare feet into them. The fabric and the rubber dried quickly in the sun, making them perfect for the occasional wading required for beaching and shoving off the canoe and for dragging it through shallow spots. He had brought along a pair of soft leather moccasins for walking around the campsite in the evening.

Eric pulled the laces of his sneakers tight and tied them. Then he got to his feet, glanced at their tent, and decided to let Robbie sleep a few minutes more. His brother had talked until almost midnight, hours beyond his normal bedtime. He had kept pestering Eric about the men dynamiting the fish until Eric had finally told him to shut up.

Robbie had sulked for a while, but soon enough the chattering machine was going again. How deep was the river? "Not deep," Eric had replied. Deep enough to drown in? "You can drown in two inches of water if you're lying facedown," Eric had said. Robbie looked concerned. "Don't worry," Eric had reassured him. "We'll be wearing life jackets." And on and on. Finally, Eric had ordered Robbie to go to sleep and, thankfully, he had.

Eric hadn't wanted to take Robbie on this trip in the first place. But if they were going to spend nearly a week together, Eric was going to make sure Robbie's annoying habits—the questions, the chattering, the goofy jokes only an eleven-year-old could think were funny—were kept to a minimum.

Eric hadn't been such a pest when he was eleven—no matter what anyone said. A couple of weeks ago, Eric and his dad were helping Grandpa put in new gutters on his house, and Robbie was fooling around and getting in the way, as usual. Eric was just starting to gripe about him when John Douglas cut him off, saying, "You were the same way at eleven." Eric had started to argue, but Dad said, "Sorry, son, it's true." Then Grandpa said to Eric's father, "So were you," and they started laughing. Eric hadn't thought it was so funny.

Eric walked across to the road and down to the rocky bar by the river. He skipped a stone over the gently moving water, then sat down on the rocks, hugging his knees, listening to the stillness of the woods.

The old pickup truck was gone from the riverbank, and the three men and their rowboat with it. Eric had heard their return during the night. There were muffled voices that carried easily through the quiet of the night, the scraping sound of the boat being dragged to the truck, the clank of hefting it into the bed of the truck, then the roar of the engine and the sound of them leaving.

Eric gazed up and down the Buffalo. It was neither wide nor deep. He could have thrown a rock to the opposite bank from his sitting position without much effort. He could have waded across, probably not getting any deeper than his waist. He decided that he liked mornings on camping trips best of all. The air was cool and clean. The world was silent, hardly a sign of life, except for the occasional bird out for the first snack of the day, the gentle splash of a fish flopping in the river, a woodchuck zipping around in search of breakfast.

"Better get moving," Eric said to himself. He got to his feet and headed back up the road to the campsite.

Eric walked across to the canoe, which was resting upside down over their food and gear to protect everything in case of rain. He tipped the canoe right side up, then opened the box of gear, lifted out a small one-burner stove and an aluminum pot, and got a carton of tea bags out of the food box. He carried everything around to the front of the tent. After placing the stove on a flat rock, Eric primed and lit it, then walked to a nearby pump with the pot to get water. Coming back, he watched two birds zooming low, seeming to play tag. Eric put the pot of water on the stove and sat down.

When the water was bubbling to a boil, Eric took a couple of tea bags from the carton and dropped them into the water. Then he got to his feet and walked across to the tent.

"C'mon, Robbie, rise and shine. Up and at 'em."

His brother's first response was dead silence. Then there was a long, low "Uhhhnnn-huh."

Eric bent and lifted the flap, then poked his head inside the tent. He saw a lump in the sleeping bag that was Robbie, balled up, with his head covered.

"Up, up, up," Eric said, reaching in and giving the lump a shake.

Robbie crawled out of the sleeping bag, then out of the tent, and stood up, rubbing his eyes. He was wearing only his undershorts.

"You'd better put some pants on," Eric said. As Robbie ducked back inside the tent, Eric added, "And grab your shoes while you're in there."

"Okay, okay, I will."

Eric shook his head. This was the way it was going to be all week—telling Robbie everything that he needed to do. Well, he didn't want his kid brother to cut his foot on a sharp rock before they even got under way.

Eric sat down and poured himself a cup of the steaming tea. It looked strong, which was good. He tried a sip and found it too hot to drink.

Then Robbie, pants on and shoes held in his right hand, was standing in front of him.

"Want some tea?"

"No. Can I have a soda?"

"We don't have any."

Robbie sat down and started pulling on his shoes. "We can get one at the machine in front of the store over there."

"No, no soda for breakfast."

"Well, I just thought . . ."

Eric shook his head as Robbie let the words trail off. "And there won't be any sodas along the way, either, you know." Cradling the cup of hot tea in both hands, he tried another sip and watched his brother finish tying his shoes.

"I'm hungry," Robbie said.

"Okay." Eric put down the cup and got to his feet. "C'mon."

Robbie followed Eric to the collection of boxes and gear next to the canoe. Eric bent over the ice chest and removed the lid.

"Here, take this"—three eggs—"and be careful, and this"—a skillet—"and I'll be right behind you."

Robbie stared at the eggs, frowning. "I thought you said we'd have pancakes for breakfast on the camping trip."

"We will, but today we're going to eat these eggs so we won't have to carry them along and take a chance on them breaking. These are our last eggs for a week."

"I could go without eggs for a year without any trouble."

"Go on. I'll get the spatula and the bacon and the bread."

Eric squatted next to the camp stove and put the skillet on the flame. Robbie dropped down next to him, sitting cross-legged, and watched. Eric cooked the bacon first, lifting the crisp slices from the skillet to the two aluminum plates. Next, he poured out most of the grease, and then cracked the three eggs into the skillet. Moving the spatula easily, he scrambled the eggs, then divided them between the two aluminum plates. He dropped two pieces of bread into the hot skillet, quickly turned them, and transferred the two pieces of toast to the plates.

Robbie squinted at the food on the plate in his hand. "You got some egg on the toast," he said.

"It won't kill you."

"I don't like eggs much, you know."

"By the time we're eating lunch, you'll be glad you ate this breakfast."

Robbie took the fork Eric handed him and poked at the eggs, then the toast. He decided to begin with a bite of bacon.

Eric put a small pot of water on the stove for dishwashing and sat back down to eat his food. "Eat it all," he told Robbie. "I don't want to hear you saying you're hungry in an hour."

After breakfast, Eric washed the utensils, and Robbie—to Eric's surprise—dried them without being asked. Then they packed everything into boxes and bags, rolled up and tied their sleeping bags, and struck the tent and folded and tied it tightly.

Eric leaned over the empty canoe, took hold of a strut, and lifted the craft smoothly to a position over his head.

Robbie, watching, said, "Do you need any help?"

"I can carry it okay, but if you'll hold the back, it'll help balance it."

"I've got it."

"Okay."

They carried the canoe across the campground to the road and down to the riverbank.

"Now for the stuff," Eric said, leading the way back to the campsite.

He struggled with the box of gear, then the box of food. Each was a heavy load for one person. Robbie, in two trips, brought the sleeping bags and the tent.

When everything was moved, the two of them made a final inspection of the campsite to make sure that nothing had been left behind or was littering the place.

"It looks like nobody even camped here," Robbie said.

Eric grinned. "That's the way it's supposed to look when you leave a campsite."

Back at the river, they loaded everything into the canoe—between the struts—tied it all in place, and put on their life jackets.

The sun was up now, giving added confirmation that a hot day was in the making.

Eric shoved the canoe across the rocks and halfway into the water. "Okay, go ahead and step in. Take the seat at the front."

Robbie got into the rear of the canoe and half-climbed, half-stepped across the gear to the forward seat while Eric held the craft steady. Robbie sat down, turned with a grin, and picked up a paddle.

Eric skidded the canoe farther into the water and followed it, standing in water up to his calves. Then he stepped in and quickly sat down in the aft seat. He picked up a paddle and used it to shove off.

The canoe glided toward the middle of the narrow river, moving downstream.

Eric took a deep stroke on the right side to straighten their path.

"We're off!" Robbie shouted from his seat at the front.

"Yes," Eric said, not quite as happily, "we are."

CHAPTER 3

LUCAS was the first one awake, at a few minutes after ten in the morning. He, Wilmer, and Jerry had been up almost until daylight cleaning the fish they'd caught earlier in the evening, while Jerry's wife, Dorothy, wrapped and packed them away in the large freezer in the garage. It had been a good haul, better even than Jerry had promised. Lucas reminded himself that before he and his brother left Jerry's place for good, they would have to get some ice to pack around their share of the fish. Probably that general store they'd passed on the way here would have some.

Lucas threw back the light blanket and lifted himself into a sitting position on the floor where he had slept. A wooden floor covered with linoleum did not make the best bed in the world, and he felt stiff all over. He glanced at Wilmer, asleep on the sofa. Lucas and his brother had flipped a coin for the sofa, and Wilmer had won. He always was the lucky one.

Lucas got to his feet and stretched his arms over his head. It felt good. He looked at the door to his left. Not a sound. Jerry and Dorothy were still asleep. No wonder—they had their bed.

Barefoot and buckling his trousers, Lucas walked into the kitchen and looked around. He went across to the stove and picked up the coffeepot, an old tin dripolator. The coffee grounds from the day before were still in the top, and with a shake, he confirmed that some coffee remained in the bottom. He took the coffeepot to the back door, dumped the contents on the ground, and returned.

Then he began searching through the cabinets for a can of coffee, slamming each door as he went.

"What's all the racket?"

Lucas looked up at Wilmer standing in the doorway, rubbing his eyes.

"I can't find any coffee."

"Well, don't look at me. I don't know where they keep it."

"Anyplace else, I'd just drive downtown and get a cup of coffee. But Gilbert hasn't got a downtown."

Wilmer grinned. "That's right, and that's good. Didn't I tell you this was the perfect place? Hardly any people at all, and the folks who are here all mind their own business."

"We should've gone on back up to Yellville last night when we finished the fish."

"It was almost dawn."

"Yeah, but at least I'd be able to find a cup of coffee."

Lucas tried another cabinet, found a can of coffee, and lifted it out with a grunt of satisfaction.

After he had poured water into the pot and measured the coffee out into the basket and placed the pot on a burner, he turned back to his brother. "You'd better go and wake up Jerry. We've got to call St. Louis."

Wilmer didn't move. "We don't need Jerry to call St. Louis."

Lucas watched Wilmer for a moment. Wilmer might be the one with all the luck, but he wasn't the one with all the brains. "Look," he said, as if explaining something for the sixteenth time, "Jerry lives here. He's the one who owns that land over there with the barn on it, and he owns all the tools. We need him. So we want him to feel that he's in on everything. Can you understand that?"

Wilmer shrugged without answering, then turned and walked through the living room, toward the bedroom door.

Lucas listened to the coffee percolating and reflected that this was just about the best deal he'd ever found for himself. In that big barn that Jerry owned on a whole bunch of acres of trees and empty country, a long way from any road, they stripped down stolen cars, taking out anything that would sell: radios, air-conditioning units, tape decks, air bags, mufflers, bumpers, hubcaps—the list was huge. The cars came in mostly from Arkansas and Missouri, but sometimes from as far away as Oklahoma and Tennessee. The men in St. Louis who provided the cars also picked up the parts. The work was hard, but that was nothing new to Lucas. Unlike his brother, Lucas had worked hard all his life. But even Wilmer had his uses when Lucas was there to make him keep moving. Most important, Lucas was his own boss, and he was raking in a lot of money.

He was pouring a cup of coffee when Wilmer reappeared in the doorway, grinning. "They're trying to wake up."

Lucas, Wilmer, and Jerry were finishing their late breakfast of bacon, eggs over easy, and toast. Dorothy was at the sink, running the hot water and getting ready to wash the dishes.

Lucas shoved his plate away and glanced at her. He knew that she didn't like him. She never looked at him, never joked, hardly ever spoke at all. Well, that was okay with him. Lucas didn't like her either. What worried him was that maybe she acted that way because she didn't approve of Jerry's getting mixed up with him and Wilmer.

Lucas tried to avoid talking business in front of her. The less she knew, the better, he figured. But sometimes, like now, it couldn't be helped.

"St. Louis says there're a couple of cars coming in tomorrow evening, and a truck to haul out some parts."

"They'd better be bringing in some money too," Wilmer said.

Lucas looked at his brother. "Don't they always?" Then he looked at Jerry. "So Wilmer and me, we'll go on up to Yellville for the night, and then we'll be back here tomorrow afternoon."

Jerry nodded and grinned. Jerry grinned too much for Lucas's taste. But since he owned the barn and the tools, Lucas never said anything about it.

Dorothy began picking up the dishes from the table, not looking at anyone.

"Better fix some food for us to take to the barn. It's going to be a long night, and maybe a long day after that."

"Dorothy will fix some."

Lucas watched Jerry's wife scraping dishes and sliding them into the hot water in the sink. She didn't show any sign of enthusiasm about her assignment, but she didn't protest.

Then, to his surprise, she spoke. Without looking at them, she said, "Jerry, you'd better talk to them about what I told you last night."

Lucas's right eyebrow went up a notch. What was this all about?

"Yeah," Jerry said. "Dorothy pointed out that now with summer coming on, there's going to be a lot of traffic on the river, a lot. There'll be more canoes than you can count, and campers and fishermen and hikers all over the place."

Lucas frowned. "So?"

"It's just that we worked all winter without having hardly nobody around, but it ain't going to be that way during the summer."

"Is that a problem?"

"It could be."

Wilmer piped up, "I don't see any problem."

"Wait a minute." Lucas waved off Wilmer. "You mean like those boys we saw down on the river last night?"

"Yeah, only there's going to be lots and lots of them, and not all of them stay on the river all the time. Some of them go tromping around all over the place. They're collecting leaves and trying to spot birds—all kinds of tourist things."

"Maybe tromping right up to the door of the barn," Lucas said. "Is that what you mean?"

"Yep." Jerry was bobbing his head in that funny way he had of nodding. "Two, three years ago, I caught a couple of 'em on my land, painting my barn."

Wilmer sat with a puzzled expression on his face. "What color were they painting it?"

Jerry snorted into his coffee cup.

"They weren't putting paint on the barn, you dope!" said Lucas, shaking his head in disbelief at his brother's ignorance. "He means they were painting pictures of the barn—though why anybody'd want to do a thing like that is beyond me."

"Anyway, I ran 'em off," Jerry announced proudly.

Lucas looked at Dorothy and frowned. She was concentrating on wiping a plate with a sponge. Advice from Dorothy had a way of rubbing against the grain with Lucas. Maybe she was just trying to get them to shut down the operation at the barn, and Jerry was dumb enough to go along with her.

"Yeah," Lucas said slowly. "I'll give it some thought."

CHAPTER 4

BY noon, the boys were past Red Bluff, almost four miles downstream, according to Eric's calculations. When it was time to stop for lunch, Eric aimed the canoe toward a rocky bar on the right, just beyond Brush Creek. The bar extended into the stream, a good bet to catch whatever breeze there was. Those cozy-looking inlets made pretty scenes for picture postcards, but they harbored too many mosquitoes and other biting insects to offer good camping. Better to be out on a point where the breezes were blowing.

"Ready to eat?" he called out.

"Yes," Robbie said without turning around. He was riding with his paddle resting on the gunwales.

After a splashy and noisy start, Robbie's enthusiasm for paddling had waned, then suddenly reawakened, only to wane again, time after time. When

Robbie was thrashing the water with his paddle, Eric concerned himself mainly with steering, moving around a rock here and there, keeping the canoe on a straight path in the middle of the stream. They made better time when Robbie was resting and Eric paddled, but Eric said nothing. He had learned from his father that canoeing mountain streams was not a sport of speed. The point of it all was to see the river, the bluffs, the woods, the occasional wild animal, and to enjoy all of it.

When they'd passed a small creek on the right emptying into the Buffalo, Eric reached into the pocket of a pack and took out a folded map encased in a clear plastic envelope. He laid his paddle across the gunwales and looked at the map.

"That's Bear Creek on the right," he told Robbie.

Robbie turned and looked at him. "Really?" he said. "Are there bears in there?"

"No. No bears."

Eric leaned forward and replaced the map in the pack, then picked up his paddle and stroked.

Robbie was still watching him. "Then why do they call it Bear Creek?"

"Who knows?"

"There must be bears in there."

"Well, this is the Buffalo River, and you haven't seen any buffalo, have you?"

"No." Robbie seemed unconvinced.

"So, turn around and paddle."

They moved through pools, shallows, and short stretches of swift-running drops that rippled in a gentle imitation of white-water rapids. They negotiated the turns in the meandering river, with Eric expertly using the current to help steer the canoe.

Alongside one of the deep, still pools, a long black snake lay coiled on a flat rock at the bank, sunning itself.

Eric glanced ahead at Robbie. His brother hadn't noticed the snake. Eric wondered whether he should call his attention to it. The sight of a snake in the wild might frighten him, and Eric did not want to go through almost a week of canoe camping with his kid brother dreaming of snakes hiding everywhere. Then he decided that the snake was part of the river and the woods, a part of what they had come to see.

"Robbie, over there, see the snake on the rock?"

Robbie whirled his head around, then spotted the snake and stared at it a moment. He turned and looked at Eric. "Neat," he said.

Eric smiled at him and nodded. "Yeah," he said.

When they rode the river into a flat expanse of land, with no rise in the banks on either side, the river widened out into a thin sheet of water, and the canoe scraped the rocky bottom.

Robbie tried for a moment to pole the canoe forward over the rocks, then looked back at Eric with an expression that said, What now?

Eric stepped out of the canoe into the ankle-deep water and said, "We drag."

"What?"

"C'mon, hop out. We've got to drag it through. It's part of life in a canoe on the Buffalo River."

"I'll get my shoes wet."

"They'll dry."

Robbie stepped out uncertainly onto the slippery rocks lining the bottom of the river.

After skidding the canoe about fifteen yards over the rocks, Eric was standing in water up to his knees. "Okay, I'll hold the canoe while you step in."

Robbie got into the canoe and sat down. Then Eric stepped in, seated himself, picked up his paddle, and shoved off.

Now Eric paddled the canoe to the bar, driving the bow onto the bank of small rocks. He jumped out into the knee-deep water and told Robbie, "Okay, hop out."

His brother jumped out onto the rocks.

"Now pull."

With Eric in the water and shoving from the rear and Robbie tugging on the line attached to the bow, they scooted the canoe up onto the bank.

Eric grabbed the handles of the canoe box and lifted it out of the canoe—the box doubled as a table at mealtimes.

"I'm going to go exploring," Robbie said.

Eric looked around. There was nothing but the river and the woods and the trickling sound of Brush Creek flowing into the Buffalo behind them. "Okay, but don't go far, and come when I call you."

Robbie took a couple of steps, then stopped and turned back to Eric. "Are there snakes?"

"Maybe, but it's nothing to worry about if you're careful. The snakes don't want to bump into you any more than you want to bump into them. They're not going to attack you. Just be careful not to step on one. They get mad when you do that. Watch where you walk, and you'll be all right."

Robbie hesitated, then announced, "Right," and marched off toward the woods.

Eric watched him go, a little surprised at his younger brother's confidence and fearlessness. Then he turned back to his work.

From the food box he lifted out the paper bag labeled Day 1 Lunch, then a box of crackers. He placed the containers on the canoe box. He got knives and forks out of a bag, and then a small pouch of powdered fruit juice concentrate.

When the lunch was spread out, he looked around

and realized he hadn't heard a sound from Robbie since he had disappeared into the woods. Not hearing him—not even a shouted announcement of a discovery—was unusual.

Eric frowned and walked toward the edge of the woods. "Robbie! Hey, Robbie!"

For a troubling moment, there was no reply, just the quiet of the woods and the murmur of the flowing water.

Then he heard Robbie's voice: "Coming!"

Robbie arrived carrying some leaves that had caught his fancy and a rock that looked worth keeping. "See what I found."

"Uh-huh. Lunch is ready."

"Can I keep them?"

"You've got a pack. If you want to load it up with leaves and rocks, that's okay with me."

Robbie walked over to the canoe and stuffed his newfound treasures in his pack while Eric sat on the ground next to the canoe box and opened the lunch bag.

Seating himself across from his older brother, Robbie took a bite of the peanut butter sandwich and looked with distaste at the lemon drink in his aluminum cup. "It looks like it's going to taste sour."

"It's got sugar in it."

"I wish I had a soda."

"Well, you don't. We're roughing it, remember."

Robbie took a sip, made a face, put down the cup, and turned his attention back to the sandwich. He took a bite and chewed absently, keeping his eyes fixed upstream. After he swallowed, he said, "You know what I was thinking?"

Eric didn't answer, so Robbie continued. "I was thinking we should have some kind of secret code worked out, in case we run into real trouble."

Eric rolled his eyes. "What kind of real trouble would that be?"

"I don't know," said Robbie, taking another bite of his sandwich. "A flash flood. Bear attack. An avalanche maybe."

Eric laughed. "Avalanche? I don't think so. And do you know what the odds are against a flash flood or a bear attack on this river?"

"You never know," Robbie said earnestly. "Better safe than sorry."

Eric rolled his eyes again. No way had he been this goofy when he was eleven.

"Okay, here's the code," said Robbie, draining his lemon drink. "Two taps mean 'What's the matter?' " He clinked a stone against his cup. "Three taps mean 'I'm hurt.' Two quick taps, then a pause, then another tap mean 'Get help fast.' "

"And five quick knocks on the head mean 'I am an eleven-year-old doofus,' " said Eric.

"C'mon, Eric, be serious," said Robbie.

"I am serious—you *are* an eleven-year-old doofus."

Robbie gave Eric a look that showed clearly that his feelings had been hurt.

"Okay," Eric said, relenting. "Show me that code one more time."

Happily, Robbie tapped away on his aluminum cup until they both had the code memorized. "There," he said. "Now we'll know what to do in case of a bear attack."

"Whatever," said Eric. "But right now, I think you'd better stop that banging, or you're going to need a code signal that means 'Sorry I dented your cup, Dad.' "

CHAPTER 5

ERIC and Robbie glided along a stretch of still water. The pebbly creekbed was clearly visible through a depth of about three or four feet.

It was midafternoon, the hottest part of the day, and though summer technically would not begin for another week, it felt like the middle of August to Eric. He paddled just enough to keep the canoe on course and let his mind drift, enjoying the pleasure of meandering silently down a lazy river.

Then, suddenly, Robbie sprang from his seat in the front of the canoe and belly flopped into the water, disappearing beneath the surface.

The thrust of Robbie's leap almost tipped the canoe. Only fast action by Eric—a deep stroke of the paddle—shot the wobbling canoe forward and set it back on an even course. Then, downstream of Robbie, Eric turned and looked back, to see his grinning kid brother standing in water to his waist, holding aloft in both hands a turtle with a shell the size of a dinner plate.

Furious, Eric shouted, "Robbie!"

He turned the canoe toward shore and banked it, then stepped out to watch, hands on hips, as Robbie approached through the shallow water, still holding the turtle above his head. Robbie's broad grin faded under Eric's glare.

"That was the stupidest thing I've ever seen."

"Eric, I—"

"You almost tipped us."

"I didn't mean—"

"We're lucky that everything's not floating down the river right now—our food, our sleeping bags, the tent." Eric paused. "And all you can say is that you didn't mean to."

"I'm sorry, jeez," said Robbie. "But it was hot, and I wanted a dip anyway, and when I saw the turtle, I . . ."

Eric glared silently, until Robbie figured out that he'd be better off just shutting up. "Sorry," Robbie mumbled.

"Maybe we ought to leave the river at the next take-out point, hitch a ride back to the car, and go home," said Eric.

"I said I was sorry," Robbie said. This time, he sounded to Eric as if he meant it.

Eric glared at him another moment, then said, "Okay."

"Can I keep him?"

"What?"

Robbie was holding the turtle with both hands out in front of him. The turtle had long since retreated into its shell.

Eric took a deep breath and blew the air out. "Good grief! Why would you want to keep him? That turtle would like nothing better than to bite you. But go ahead—you can keep him if he stays in your end of the canoe, and if you're willing to paddle with your feet on the gunwales."

Robbie grinned. "Thanks."

Less than an hour later, weary of keeping his feet up on the gunwales and leery of the turtle's long neck now swaying around outside the shell, Robbie announced, "Maybe I ought to let him go."

"Maybe so." Eric tried not to let his smile show.

Eric lay on his back on top of the sleeping bag, staring up into the darkness inside the tent. He heard the rhythmic chirping of crickets, the gentle murmuring of the river, and Robbie's even breathing next to him.

At the campsite last night, Robbie had chattered until almost midnight, long after Eric had wanted to drop off to sleep. But the long day of paddling in the sun, following the short night of sleep, had sent Robbie into his sleeping bag tonight before the campfire had burned down. And there hadn't been a peep out of him since.

Eric was still a little angry about the turtle. It had been a really stupid maneuver—typical Robbie. Eric might have been, as his father had said, Robbie's age at the time of his first canoe trip, but he had had enough sense not to jump out of the canoe in midstream. Eric smiled, reliving that first trip, just him and his dad.

Then his smile faded as a memory came to him, an incident that he hadn't thought about in years. He and his father had been on the Buffalo—near the very spot where Robbie had taken his plunge, in fact. While his dad was setting up camp, Eric had gotten out his pole to do a little fishing. The fish hadn't been biting, so he figured he'd set out another line, to increase his chances.

Eric squirmed in the darkness, thinking about what he'd done next.

He'd gotten his dad's pole, baited the hook and cast it, then wedged the handle of the pole under a rock on shore. After doing that, he'd gone back to casting with his own pole. The next thing he knew, his dad's pole was getting dragged into the water by a hooked fish and he was scrambling after it. Too late. The pole had disappeared into the water, gone for good.

His dad had been pretty mad, to say the least. That pole had been Grandpa's when he was a boy, and Eric would have been given it someday. Eric had felt terrible about losing it, and his dad had even threatened him with the same thing Eric had threatened Robbie with today—cutting their trip short. But John Douglas had seen fit to forgive his son, and the rest of the trip had been great. . . . Maybe, Eric thought, I should try to cut Robbie a little slack.

Eric turned onto his side on the sleeping bag and closed his eyes. Well, they had survived the episode, and maybe Robbie had learned a lesson, as Eric had that day years ago. He had to admit that his brother had been agreeable to gathering pine boughs for ground cover instead of exploring, and he had helped set up the tent. He had even cleaned up the plates after dinner. Maybe everything was going to be okay. Eric quickly fell asleep.

"Eric! Somebody is out there!"

Robbie was shaking his shoulder and speaking in a loud whisper.

"Huh?" Eric registered Robbie's words slowly. Coming awake, he lifted himself on one elbow. "Out where?"

"Listen!" Robbie's whisper seemed like a shout in the quiet of the tent.

Then Eric heard the unmistakable sound of a footfall on the dry twigs and loose rocks of the bar where they had pitched their tent. And then he heard another.

"Hear that?" Robbie whispered.

Eric suddenly felt his heart pounding furiously, but he consciously made an effort to sound calm. "Yeah, it's something all right."

They listened a moment and heard nothing further. The intruder was standing still.

Eric turned slowly and looked all around, expecting to see the glow of a flashlight outside through the tent walls. But there was nothing but darkness.

"It's probably those men," Robbie whispered.

"Nah. Why would they be walking around here in the middle of the night? That doesn't make sense." Eric wished he had been able to sound more convincing.

"You said that what they were doing was against the law. And we saw them."

"Shhhh."

There was the sound of a step, then another.

"Maybe it's a bear . . . from Bear Creek."

"Quiet, will you."

Eric rolled over, raised himself to hands and knees,

and crawled the couple of feet to the back of the tent. He opened his pack and rummaged through it until he found the flashlight. Then his hand bumped the small hand ax he carried for chopping kindling for the campfire. He lifted out the ax, too.

"What are you doing?"

"I'm going out to see what's walking around out there."

"You're going out *there*?"

Eric took a breath. "It's better than sitting in here all night and wondering, isn't it?"

Robbie didn't answer for a moment. Then he said, "Do you want me to go with you?"

Eric smiled at his younger brother in the darkness. That was the right thing to say. "No, you stay here."

Eric crawled to the front of the tent and paused a moment, hoping for another footfall outside to give him a bearing on the whereabouts of the intruder.

"What's the matter?" Robbie asked.

"Wait a minute. Listen."

There was the sound of a step, and then the tent shook slightly. The intruder had bumped into one of the rear guylines.

Neither boy spoke.

Eric unzipped the screen at the front of the tent and leapt out, turning. He had the ax in his right hand

and the flashlight in his left. He flicked the switch on the flashlight and aimed the beam of light across the top of the tent.

A cow turned its head and stared indifferently into the beam of light.

Eric felt a wave of relief. He took a deep breath, puffed out his cheeks, and exhaled. Then he shook his head and chuckled. He felt like a fool standing there with an ax in his hand, looking at a cow.

"Eric?" Robbie was no longer whispering, but he spoke softly.

"C'mon out and take a look at our mysterious visitor."

"Is it all right?"

"C'mon. No problem."

Robbie pushed aside the screen netting and crawled out. He got to his feet and followed the beam of the flashlight to the cow's face. "A cow?" he said.

"Yeah. I guess it belongs to somebody who lives around here. Well, let's get it out of here. We don't want it tripping on a rope and falling in on us during the night."

"How do we make it go away?"

Eric bent down, picked up several small rocks, then lobbed them at the cow. The cow blinked at the stones hitting its flank, then turned in a leisurely fashion and ambled into the woods.

Back in the tent, with the screen netting zipped and the flashlight and ax put away, Robbie said, "I still think you were brave to go out there."

"And you were brave to offer to go with me. Now, let's get back to sleep."

CHAPTER 6

THE morning haze over the river burned away quickly under the glare of the rising sun, and by the time they had eaten breakfast, washed up, struck the tent, and loaded their gear, the day was already hot.

Paddling easily in the gentle current, Eric let Robbie ride along with his paddle on the gunwales or stroke the water, whichever he liked.

"Are you going to tell Dad about the cow?" Robbie asked, turning in his seat.

"Sure. He'll get a kick out of it."

Robbie frowned. "I was really scared."

"So was I, for a minute there," said Eric. "Hey, speaking of that, what happened to your special code? That was your one chance at tapping out 'Get help fast,' and you blew it."

"Uh, well, I . . ." Robbie hesitated. He couldn't tell whether Eric was kidding him or not.

"We'll have to come up with some code for 'Beware of cow,' " said Eric, laughing.

Robbie laughed with him. "Dad'll think it's all pretty silly, won't he? I mean, he'll think that *we* were pretty silly, being scared of a cow."

"I don't think so. Hearing something walking around outside your tent in the middle of the night could be pretty serious business."

"Maybe." He turned back to the front.

Then almost immediately, he wheeled around again to look at Eric. "And—"

Eric knew what was coming, but he said, "And what?"

"Are you going to tell Dad that I jumped out of the canoe and almost tipped us?"

Eric looked at Robbie's serious face, and he thought about the time he'd lost his dad's fishing pole. When they got home and Grandpa asked what had happened to the pole he'd had as a child, Eric's dad said something about it falling in the river—not a lie, exactly, but he didn't tell Grandpa the whole truth about Eric losing it. John Douglas almost made it sound as if it had been his own fault. Eric had really appreciated his father's keeping his dumb move a secret between them.

"I won't tell Dad if you don't want me to," he said.

Robbie nodded. "Yeah," he said. "I think that would be better."

"My lips are sealed."

Their second day out went more smoothly than the first. Robbie didn't do any belly flops out of the canoe, and Eric didn't feel the need to snap at him quite so often. In late morning, they saw a fox creeping in the underbrush by the river's edge. Then, a few more miles downriver, they passed three deer—two does and a buck. The deer didn't even bound into the woods when the canoe glided past; they just stood calmly watching them. The deer in these woods, where hunting was forbidden, had become quite accustomed to seeing people. Some of them seemed almost tame. And these three appeared to be as curious about the boys as the boys were about them.

Eric and Robbie left the deer behind and paddled to the end of a trail that followed the river along the bank. Beyond the end of the trail, Eric steered the canoe toward a rocky bar for their lunch stop.

Hopping out into the shallow water, Eric shoved the front half of the canoe onto the rocks. Robbie jumped out too and began tugging at the line to help. He was learning.

As Eric waded onto the bank, Robbie was already turning and setting his sights on the woods for a few minutes of exploring.

"Don't go far," Eric said.

"Okay."

"Call me if you run into a cow."

Robbie turned and grinned at Eric, and then he was gone.

For a moment, Eric stood and watched the river, shallow and swift-running at this point. In the quiet of the woods, he could hear the soft rippling of the water. The noonday sun was hot, but there was a pleasant breeze coming in from the water. Farther down the river, in a pool of deeper water, he saw a fish jump.

Eric lifted the food box out of the canoe and put it down on the rocks. He opened the box and took out the paper bag marked Day 2 Lunch, then closed the box and placed the paper bag on the lid. He got cups and spoons from the box of gear and mixed in powder from an envelope with water from a canteen, making the lemonade for lunch. All was set. Eating without cooking was the secret to a quick lunch on the river.

He walked to the edge of the woods, climbed up a small ridge, and stood between two trees on the rise in the ground. In the distance he saw Robbie standing still, looking up into the trees. He was holding a stick in one hand.

"Let's eat," Eric called out.

Robbie turned and ran toward him.

* * *

After lunch, Eric paddled hard. He wanted to put a few miles behind them as quickly as possible. Then they could stop early, allowing him to get in a couple of hours of fishing. With any luck, they would be frying fish on the camp stove tonight.

They quickly passed Spring Creek, flowing into the Buffalo from the right. Eric consulted the map, then decided to stop for the night at the first good site after he saw Water Creek flowing in from the left.

"I'll fish and you can explore," he said, explaining his plan to Robbie.

"Yeah."

"We'll stop a mile or two from the Highway Fourteen overpass. That way, we won't have to listen to the cars all night."

"Okay."

Robbie dug his paddle into the water for a few minutes. He wasn't interested in fishing, but he did like the idea of plenty of time for exploration. Eventually, he tired of the paddling, and he let Eric's deep strokes propel the canoe through the water.

As soon as Eric banked the craft, Robbie was out of it and making his way up the bar, heading toward the woods beyond.

"Wait a minute. Let's set up the tent first."

Robbie turned back from his path to the woods. "Now?" he asked.

"Now."

"You sound like Mom."

Eric grinned. "Maybe, but the first thing to do at a campsite is to set up the tent. Then if a storm blows up, you're set—instead of getting soaked while you try to set up your tent. Understand?"

Robbie looked at the cloudless sky. "It's not going to rain."

"I know, but if it does, we'll be ready. C'mon, let's get it done."

They moved out into the woods to scoop up boughs for a bed of padding between the tent floor and the round rocks on the bar.

Then in another ten minutes, the tent was up and staked.

"There, that wasn't so bad, was it?"

"I guess not."

"Don't go too far, okay?"

Robbie raced away, and Eric unloaded their gear for the night. He rolled out the sleeping bags in the tent, then turned over the canoe and stashed some of their gear under the shelter of the hull. After arranging a ring of larger rocks for a fireplace, he roamed the woods next to the bar, collecting an armload of firewood, then dumped the wood next to the fireplace.

With these chores finished, he pulled out the tackle

box and his rod and reel, changed into a swimsuit, and waded out into the water to catch their
dinner.

After an hour, Eric had four fish on the stringer—
three bream and one bass. Dinner was assured. He
had thrown back three fish too small to keep.

The sun was getting low in the sky when Eric
turned in the water and began wading toward the
bank.

With a sudden sense of alarm, he realized that he
had not seen or heard Robbie since shortly after he
began fishing. His brother had emerged from the
woods and watched from the bank as Eric made his
first couple of casts, then disappeared again.

Eric stepped onto the bar, putting down his fish
and equipment. He looked and listened. Nothing.

"Robbie!" he shouted.

Nothing.

"Kids," he mumbled to himself, half-angry with
Robbie for wandering out of earshot, half-angry with
himself for allowing it to happen.

He stripped off his swimsuit, dried himself, and
changed into his jeans, all the while telling himself
that there was nothing in the woods around the Buffalo River that might harm an eleven-year-old boy.
He hoped he was right. If nothing else, being lost was

sure to frighten Robbie. And, worse yet, darkness was falling.

After Eric finished dressing, he walked into the woods, heading in the direction he had seen Robbie take.

Lucas stepped out of the passenger side of the pickup truck and moved aside to let Wilmer get out. Then he slammed the door as Wilmer ran to the barn door, a key ring in his hand. Wilmer selected a key, inserted it in the large padlock, and turned it. The padlock came open and he removed it and swung the barn door open.

Jerry drove the truck into the barn and Lucas followed him inside. Wilmer was closing the door behind them by the time Jerry climbed out of the pickup and walked over to Lucas.

"Get that generator going," Lucas called out to his brother. "It's going to be dark before long."

"Sure."

Lucas watched Wilmer scurry to the back of the barn. His brother might not be the smartest man in the world, but Lucas had to admit that Wilmer had stumbled onto the perfect place for their operation. Wilmer had run into Jerry in a bar in Yellville one night. They fell into conversation, and when Jerry mentioned owning a barn set deep in the woods, bells went off in Wilmer's brain. Lucas was skeptical at first—he was always skeptical of Wilmer's ideas—but he knew the place was right the instant he saw it. It was a mile or more off the river on one side and a mile or more off Highway 14 on the other side. Hills and woods surrounded it. Nobody lived anywhere near. What passed for a road from the highway to the barn was barely recognizable as such—more like a path between trees. There was nobody to see the lights when they worked all night, or when the boys came to pick up a load, and nobody to hear the noise of their work and wonder about it. The place was perfect. Talking Jerry into coming in on the deal was a snap. His wife was another matter, but she finally came around.

Jerry looked across at Lucas and said, "Do you think they might want to take some tires?"

Lucas glanced at the tires stacked against the far wall. There were a lot of them, maybe a hundred. Jerry was always worrying about the growing collection of tires. "You know that they never want tires," Lucas said. "Who'd buy a used tire?"

"We've got to do something. I'm going to wind up with a barn full of old tires, and someday somebody is going to ask where they all came from."

Lucas eyed the piles of tires. By the time the barn was filled with old tires, he and Wilmer were going to be long gone, spending their money down in Texas or out in California. He said, "Maybe you can start carrying them out a few at a time in the pickup."

"But where'll I take them?"

Lucas gave a little laugh. "There're plenty of hills around here. Maybe you can just roll 'em down a hill."

"Dorothy says that when you and Wilmer pull out, I'm going to be left with the problem."

"If Dorothy is so smart, maybe she can think of something to do with them."

Jerry didn't answer. He looked at the piles of tires for a minute, then went over to the far wall and threw a switch. The barn was bathed with light.

CHAPTER 7

THE white tail flickered in the shadows, once, twice, and then the deer bounded forward, disappearing around a bend in the trail. Robbie ran after it, keeping low to the ground, trying to make as little noise as possible. His sneakers crunched over the fallen leaves that littered the hiking trail. He wished he could run through the forest more quietly, like an old-time trapper, or like Indians did in the movies. If he had been wearing moccasins, he would have been able to move silently—he was sure of it.

Up ahead, Robbie could see the deer pause. He had been pursuing it for quite some time. If the deer had really wanted to get away, Robbie knew, it could easily have outdistanced him. But, like the deer they'd seen from the river earlier in the day, this buck did not seem overly concerned by the presence of people.

When Robbie got too close to it, the deer would spring away. But it was too lazy, or too unconcerned, to run far, and it even stayed on the hiking trail, where it was easier to move. Robbie had been able to track it simply by following the trail, and even now, in the fading light of dusk, he was able to continue pursuing it.

He crept along the path, wishing once again that he was wearing soft moccasins instead of sneakers. The buck was in the trail up ahead, nibbling casually at some new green grass shoots growing alongside a fallen log. Robbie was determined to get closer to the deer. He dropped down into a crouch, then proceeded on all fours, moving as smoothly and silently as he possibly could. The buck watched him out of the corner of its eye.

When he was twenty-five feet from the deer, it suddenly bounded away, leaving the trail this time, as if it had finally grown weary of the game. Robbie watched, disappointed, as the deer dashed through the trees, disappearing into the gathering darkness.

"Hey, come back," Robbie said quietly, knowing he'd seen the last of that deer.

He looked around and realized with a start that the sun had set and that he was alone in the forest, with no food, water, or shelter. And he was unsure of how to get back to camp—the trail had branched at several points. He doubted he'd be able to retrace his steps, especially in the dark.

What to do?

His dad had told him once that if he ever got lost, he should stay where he was—it's easier to find someone if he's not wandering around.

On the other hand, Robbie knew that if he made his way downhill, he'd eventually find the river. Then he'd be able to find Eric. But the trail had gone up and down several hills, so figuring out which way was the real downhill direction wouldn't be as simple as it sounded. And even if he found the river, he wouldn't know whether to turn upstream or down to find Eric.

Maybe it would be best to stay put. Eric would find him eventually, wouldn't he?

Sure he would.

Probably . . . Robbie hoped.

As he stood on the trail debating with himself, Robbie realized he could see dim lights shining through the trees in the far distance. Could they be . . . But maybe they were just stars shining through the branches. He looked straight up, at the stars overhead, then down again at the lights through the trees. Yes, they were definitely brighter than stars!

Robbie didn't know whether the lights were in somebody's house or at a gas station or along a lighted stretch of highway. But wherever they were, they meant people, and people meant he wasn't lost anymore.

Eric quick-stepped up the trail. He stopped and cupped his hands around his mouth. "Robbie!" he called. After a few seconds, a faint echo came back to him: *Robbie.* Then nothing, just the slight breeze rustling the treetops and the occasional squawk or twitter of a bird, the skittering of a squirrel or chipmunk.

Eric hiked on up the trail. Soon he came to a fork. Hmmm . . . if I were an eleven-year-old, which way would I go? he asked himself.

He peered along the left-hand side. It turned sharply up the slope of a hill, then petered out abruptly about thirty yards ahead, in a tumble of boulders.

Eric looked the other way. The path to the right skirted along the base of the hill, rising and dipping gently. If there was any chance of finding Robbie before the last light faded, he would have to assume that his brother had taken the path of least resistance— literally. "Okay, let's go," Eric said to himself, then turned to the right and trotted down the path, calling, "Robbie! Hey, Robbie!" into the dusk.

* * *

Lucas walked toward the automobile parts and accessories stacked against the far wall of the barn. There were radios, cassette players, mufflers, wheel rims, air bags, rearview mirrors, even fenders and bumpers.

"A nice little inventory," he said, more to himself than to either Wilmer or Jerry. He tried for a moment to calculate the value of everything. He couldn't do it. Then he thought about the money that was coming in tonight to pay for all these items. But there was no way of estimating the amount. It depended on what they took.

"You better hightail it out to the highway to meet them," Lucas told Wilmer. "It's going to be pitch-dark before long, and the boys don't like sitting around in hot cars."

"Aw, they won't be here for a couple of hours at least," Wilmer said.

Lucas just stared at him.

"I went last time," Wilmer went on. "Why can't Jerry go?"

Lucas continued to watch him without speaking.

Finally, Jerry said, "I'll go. There's nothing to do around here anyway."

Wilmer grinned at Lucas and nodded.

"Okay," Lucas said. It didn't really matter which of them took the pickup truck out to the highway to lead the drivers through the woods to the barn. Then he turned back to Wilmer and said, "C'mon, I'm going to find something for you to do."

Jerry walked to the barn door and swung it open. Then he stepped outside and walked several yards in a semicircle, looking around.

Wilmer watched him and said, "He does that every time. Who's he think he's going to see?"

"He's just cautious. C'mon, you can start sorting some of this stuff."

Jerry, satisfied that the way was clear, walked back into the barn, climbed into the pickup, and backed out.

"Get the door," Lucas told Wilmer.

Wilmer shrugged and walked toward the door. But as Jerry and the truck disappeared into the woods, he stopped in the doorway, tipped his head a little to one side, and said, "Hear that?"

"What?"

"It sounded like somebody shouting."

"I didn't hear anything."

"Well, I did."

"Not very likely that anybody'd be out around here, it getting dark and all. Maybe it was somebody on the river."

"A mile away?"

"When the wind's right, sounds can carry. Now come on, close the door and start sorting those things, like I told you."

Wilmer shrugged again and pulled the door shut.

Chapter 8

ROBBIE pressed himself against the side of the barn. He was breathing heavily. He felt like his heart was in his throat. His hands were shaking a little.

He was pretty sure that the man who had walked out of the barn was one of the men Eric and he had seen dynamiting the river back at Gilbert.

It had been a close call. Following the lights of the barn through the woods, he had been just a step away from pulling open the barn door when it had swung open and the man had come out. The sight of the man's reddish hair had stopped Robbie in his tracks. He'd backed up and pressed himself against the wall around the corner, one step away from being spotted. When the red-haired man drove out of the barn in the pickup truck that had been parked at the water's edge in Gilbert, Robbie knew he had been right to be cautious.

The other two men were probably in the barn. Somebody was there—he could hear voices, but he couldn't understand what they were saying.

Robbie pressed himself harder against the wall, then stood motionless, trying to think.

Eric ran up the path, calling for Robbie, then stood still as a statue, listening. There was nothing but silence and the occasional chirping of crickets.

He felt a wave of panic as he squinted into the darkness. He had convinced himself earlier that there was nothing in the woods that would harm his brother. But if Robbie hadn't taken the easy path—if he'd decided to climb a rocky hillside, for instance—then he could easily have fallen and hurt himself—broken a bone or knocked himself out.

No way, Eric told himself. Robbie could scramble over things like a goat. But even if Robbie wasn't hurt, he was going to be frightened.

Eric did the only thing he could. He started up the trail again, shouting, "Robbie! Robbie, where are you?"

Robbie breathed slowly in and out as quietly as he could. He didn't want the men inside the barn to hear him.

Then, suddenly, from a long way off, Robbie heard Eric calling him. His heart started pounding, from happiness this time instead of fear. He was saved— or was he?

He couldn't shout back, because that would bring the men out of the barn. And Robbie certainly didn't want to do that.

Then he heard a man speaking. The words were clear this time, coming from just around the corner. The man was probably standing in the doorway. He had heard Eric's call. The other man said something Robbie couldn't understand.

Robbie continued to stay motionless, his breath now coming in short gasps. He squeezed his eyes shut, then opened them. Finally, he heard the scraping sound of the barn door being closed.

Robbie let out a long breath. More than anything, he wanted to sit down. His legs felt shaky. He took a deep breath and tried to think.

How could he find Eric in the dark, without calling after him and alerting the men in the barn? And even if he did get to Eric, would they be able to find their way back to the camp?

Robbie took a quick glance around and decided to quit asking himself questions. He had to figure out what to do.

First, of course, he needed to get away from the

barn. One of the men might come out for something and walk around the corner. Or the red-haired man might return in the truck and spot him. He had to get himself into the woods, where he could shout an answer to Eric. Then they would find each other. Even if the men heard the shouts and came after them, they would escape in the dark. And Eric would know how to get back to the camp—Robbie was sure he would.

Robbie listened at the wall of the barn for a moment—for a voice or a footstep, which would mean one of the men was coming out the doorway. He heard an occasional murmur of conversation, otherwise nothing.

Then he broke into a run—a funny-looking run since he was trying to be quiet and quick at the same time—and didn't stop until he reached a large tree about twenty yards from the barn. From there, he leaned out and looked back at the barn. Nobody was coming after him. The lights were visible in the cracks between the boards. But there was no other sign of life.

Robbie stood still behind the tree a moment, hoping that Eric would call again and he'd be able to tell which direction he ought to go, even if he couldn't shout a response.

*   *   *

Another wave of panic swept over Eric as he stumbled along the trail. If he didn't find Robbie soon, they'd be separated till morning. Even though it was June, the nights got pretty cold. Could Robbie survive the night without shelter?

For that matter, could Eric? He was pretty sure he would be able to find his way back to camp in this darkness. Yeah, pretty sure—but not positive. He might be no better off than Robbie at this point.

Eric turned to shout again, then noticed lights in the distance. Maybe Robbie had seen them, too, and had gone to them—whatever they were.

Eric shouted, "Hey, Robbie, are you there?" and ran toward the lights.

Robbie stood behind the tree near the barn, waiting for Eric to call again.

He thought he heard something from the direction of the barn—maybe one of the men coming out—and he carefully leaned around and peered into the darkness.

Then he heard Eric shout, "Hey, Robbie, are you there?" Before Robbie could react, he saw the dim figure of his brother dashing across the field, toward the barn.

No! Don't go over there! Robbie screamed silently,

willing Eric away from the barn. *I'm over here, over here!*

Eric turned the corner of the barn, pulled the door open, and went inside.

CHAPTER 9

ERIC recognized the two men, and he was sure that they recognized him.

They must have heard him approach, because they were standing and facing the door when he opened it. He noticed that one of the men—the larger one—was holding a tire iron. They did not look friendly.

He looked from one to the other, then focused on the larger man. "I need some help," he said.

The man said, "You sure do."

The other man chuckled and then said, "What are we going to do, Lucas?"

"Be quiet. I'm thinking."

Eric looked around the barn. What had appeared at first glance to be piles of junk, maybe the remains of wrecked cars, now looked like orderly stacks of automobile parts and accessories—all of them new or close to it, not rusted and old. He wasn't sure what he was looking at, but he had an idea. He'd heard his uncle, who was a policeman in Fayetteville, talk about chop shops—places where criminals dismantled stolen cars and then sold the parts. Either this barn was an awfully strange auto-parts store or these men were using it as a chop shop. Eric had a bad feeling that he wasn't in an auto-parts store.

He turned his gaze back to the man with the tire iron, trying to keep his face a blank, trying to convey the impression that he knew nothing of what he had seen and had no interest in what was stacked all around the barn.

"Where's the little boy?" Lucas asked.

"That's the problem—he's lost. He went off exploring in the woods while I was fishing, and now I can't find him and it's dark."

"So he's somewhere out there looking for you while you're looking for him."

"I guess so." Then, his face as expressionless as possible, he added, "Can you help me?"

"I don't think so."

Eric watched the man without speaking. Jumping them both was out of the question. The one named Lucas was larger than he was—and then there was the second man. Also, there was that tire iron in Lucas's hand. Eric weighed the possibility of turning and running. No, he'd probably never make it through the door.

"We've got to do something, Lucas. There's no telling when Jerry will be back with the boys."

"Shut up, Wilmer."

Eric stood and waited. Jerry must be the third man he and Robbie had seen at Gilbert, the one with red hair. And he was on his way, making it three against one. If Jerry was bringing people here, the odds were getting even worse. Eric thought about whether he ought to make a move while the count was only two against one. Maybe he could get the tire iron away from Lucas and take out both of them. No, that only happened on television.

Maybe the best thing to do would be to try and leave casually, as if he suspected nothing. Maybe they'd just let him go.

"Well, I can see you fellows are busy," Eric said, smiling and heading toward the door. "I'll just be—"

"You're not going anywhere, kid," said Lucas, stepping in front of him.

"What?" Eric tried his best to make the question sound innocent. "Why—"

"We can't let you go stumbling around in the woods in the middle of the night, can we, Wilmer?" Lucas looked at his brother, who shook his head no.

"You might get hurt." He slapped his palm with the tire iron. "Or something."

Eric gave it one last try. "That's okay, I've really got to find my brother." He tried to step between the two men. "I'm sure I'll be all—"

"I said, you're not going no place." Lucas clamped a hand down hard on Eric's shoulder and squeezed. "Got it?"

Eric nodded. "Yeah, sure. Maybe I'll stay."

"Good. Wilmer, show the boy some hospitality."

As Lucas unclamped his hand, Wilmer grasped Eric's upper arm. Lifting it up, so that Eric had to walk almost on tiptoe, Wilmer marched him toward the back of the barn.

Robbie stood and stared through the deepening darkness at the barn, with slivers of light shining through the cracks between the boards. Even after this short a time—maybe ten minutes—he knew that his brother wasn't coming back out. Those men were crooks—Eric had said so—and he had walked in on them. Now they were holding him. Maybe they had tied him up or knocked him out—or worse.

Robbie squatted down in front of the tree and then dropped into a sitting position, leaning forward, hugging his knees.

What to do?

He should go for help—but where? He didn't know where he was or which way to go. Stumbling around in the woods in the dark did not seem like a good idea. He'd only get himself more lost than he already was, and then he wouldn't even know where the barn was.

Besides, the idea of moving away from Eric, leaving him alone with those men, bothered him. Knowing that he was close to his brother felt better.

Maybe Eric would get free somehow, and he would be on hand to help, and then they would get away together in the darkness.

"We should've gagged him," Wilmer said.

Lucas glanced at the door to the equipment room in the corner of the barn. "No need to. He knows that if he hollers, nobody is going to hear him. All that'll happen is that we'll gag him then. Naw, he'll be quiet."

"I don't know, Lucas. We should have bound him at least."

"Shut up. I'm thinking."

Wilmer stood silently for a moment, then said, "What about the little brother?"

Lucas looked at Wilmer. "That's what I'm thinking about." He grinned and added, "Wilmer, you do think sometimes, don't you?"

Wilmer frowned, straightened himself, and looked for a moment as if he was going to speak. Then he sat down and waited.

Lucas rubbed his chin. "The little brother isn't a problem at all, unless . . ." He paused and let Wilmer dangle as he waited for the explanation.

Wilmer said, "Unless?"

Lucas looked at him. "If he sees the lights in the barn, he'll probably walk right in here, just like his older brother. He's lost, and he's looking for help. No problem at all. We just put him in there with his brother."

"But you said 'unless.' "

Lucas grinned, seeming pleased that Wilmer still didn't see the point. Maybe Wilmer could think sometimes, but he couldn't think all the time. "Unless," he said slowly, "he saw his big brother come in here, and then didn't see him come back out. Then he knows there's trouble, and maybe that's trouble for us."

Wilmer frowned and nodded.

"C'mon," Lucas said, picking up a flashlight from the table. "Let's see if little brother is out there hanging around."

"Aw, wait a minute, Lucas. He's not out there. He's probably two, three miles away, off somewhere else."

Lucas glared at Wilmer. "What's the matter? You

afraid he's going to jump you in the dark? He's just a little kid."

"It's not that. . . ."

Yes, Lucas knew it wasn't that. Wilmer was afraid of the woods in the dark. He jumped at every shadow, sure it was some animal wanting to bite him.

Wilmer finally took a breath, gave a little nod, and said, "Okay."

Robbie, sitting cross-legged next to the tree, scrambled to his feet when he heard the scraping sound of the door being opened and then saw a widening beam of light shining through the doorway. For a moment he stood motionless, listening to the pounding of his heart. Then he stepped carefully out of sight, pressing his back to the rough bark, fists clenched.

He saw nothing but darkness, heard nothing. Slowly, he turned, bent, and looked around the tree.

Two men were standing together in the light from the doorway, facing each other. One of them—the larger one—was talking, and the other one was nodding his head. They both had flashlights. Robbie couldn't see their faces well, but he was sure they were the other two men he and Eric had seen on the riverbank at Gilbert.

Had they spotted him or heard him, and were they now coming to get him?

The two men turned and separated, the larger one walking away from Robbie, toward the far side of the barn and the other man walking straight toward him!

The beam from the approaching man's flashlight danced through the darkened woods, and Robbie pulled back behind the tree. In the silence, he heard the occasional cracking sound of a footstep snapping a twig. It seemed the man was moving slowly.

After a moment, the beam of light no longer splashed around the woods. Had the man turned the flashlight off? That didn't make sense. Then the sound of the footsteps stopped. All was quiet; all was dark.

Had the man returned to the barn?

Robbie waited, then leaned around the tree. He saw the man standing still, the flashlight pointed downward, illuminating his legs, feet, and a small circle of ground.

A sudden hoarse shout from the distance broke the silence. "Wilmer!"

Robbie jerked himself back behind the tree. He was just in time. The beam of the flashlight suddenly swept the woods, passing over the tree Robbie was standing behind.

"I'm coming," the man nearest Robbie called out.

Robbie looked to his left, in the direction of the

first shout, and saw a flashlight beam playing over the woods deep beyond the back of the barn. Then the light withdrew, out of sight.

Robbie waited. He heard nothing. The flashlight beam was gone. Carefully, he leaned around the tree. The man was walking back toward the front of the barn, keeping the flashlight beam on the ground in front of him. The other man appeared in the light from the doorway and called out, "Did you go all the way around to the back?"

"Yeah. Nothing there."

"I didn't see your light back there."

"I was behind you, Lucas."

Back inside, Lucas and Wilmer sat down across from each other at a long wooden worktable. At the far end of the table, a coffeepot on a hot plate began gurgling.

Lucas shoved back his chair, got up, walked to the end of the table, and poured himself a cup of coffee. When Wilmer saw that his brother wasn't going to pour a cup for him too, he got up and poured one for himself.

Coming back, Wilmer said, "What are we going to do with him?"

Lucas stirred the coffee to cool it. "I've been giving the situation some thought," he said.

Wilmer sat down and waited.

"First thing, when Jerry and the boys get here, we've got to fill Jerry in on what's happened—just Jerry, not the others. Understand?"

"Okay."

Lucas eyed Wilmer for a moment. Then he said, "There's no good at all that can come out of the boys going back and telling all the big shots that we had somebody walk in on us. Are you sure you understand?"

"Yeah, sure." Wilmer frowned and tilted his head slightly. "What if the little brother comes wandering in here while the boys are loading up the stuff? Then what?"

Lucas shook his head. "We can't do anything about that. If it happens, it happens, and the cat's out of the bag. For now, the thing we've got to remember is that we need to get the boys out of here and back on the road as quick as we can, and we'll just hope little brother doesn't show up."

"Uh-huh."

"But if he does, you let me handle it. Got that?"

"Yeah. Okay."

"What you've got to remember is that there's no need to let the boys know we had somebody walk in on us, if we can help it. Understand?"

"Sure."

Lucas watched Wilmer for another moment. "So you just make sure you don't let anything slip."

"All right. All right."

"When they get here, you take Jerry aside—maybe take him outside—and fill him in."

"Me?"

Lucas let out a breath. Didn't Wilmer ever catch on to anything the first time around? "I'll be watching them load and listing all the stuff they're taking, just like I always do. If you did that job, they'd steal us blind, and you know it. They know it too, so they'd wonder why I wasn't in here watching them." He waited for Wilmer's nod of understanding, then continued. "Besides, Jerry is your buddy, not mine. He'll take it better, hearing it from you. He always worries, and you've got to tell him that there's nothing to worry about."

"Well, wait a minute. . . ."

"What?"

Wilmer frowned, trying to get his thoughts in order. "Why do we have to tell Jerry anything anyway? If he don't know nothing about it, he's sure not to worry, right?"

Lucas watched Wilmer without speaking. Then he said, "It's Jerry's barn. Maybe he'll notice the door to the equipment room is closed, for the first time ever, and wonder why. Or maybe he'll want to get something out of there. We can't exactly tell him to keep his nose out of that room, now can we?"

"Guess not," Wilmer said.

"You've got to make sure that he understands there's nothing to worry about. We're going to fix the situation. Okay?"

"Nothing to worry about," Wilmer repeated.

"That's right—nothing to worry about."

"How are you planning to fix the situation?"

"I don't have it all worked out yet."

"We can't just let the kid go. He'd be back here with the sheriff in less than an hour."

"I know that."

"Then what are we going to do with him?"

"I'm thinking on it."

Wilmer took a tentative sip of his coffee, found it cool enough to drink, and took a swallow. "I've got an idea," he said, as he put the cup down on the table.

Lucas didn't answer. He just looked at Wilmer.

Wilmer grinned. "You always say my ideas aren't any good. But this is perfect. That's what you're going to say—that this is a perfect idea."

"Okay, what is it?"

Wilmer waited, enjoying the moment. Lucas waited with him.

"We take him to the river, drown him, and leave

his body in the water. We shove off his canoe and throw his paddle in the water. When he's found, it's a case of a city boy tipping his canoe and drowning. Maybe we ought to hit him on the head so it'll look like he hit a rock when he fell out of the canoe."

Lucas nodded. He did not tell Wilmer that the same idea had come to him as he was facing the boy inside the doorway. In the end, maybe that was what they would have to do. But Lucas didn't like the idea of murder. If something went wrong and they were caught, the price was higher than he wanted to pay. He had filed the idea away in his mind, hoping that a better one would come along.

"Well?" Wilmer asked, cocking his head.

"It's a possibility. But maybe we won't have to go that far."

"You got a better idea?"

Lucas took a sip of the coffee and let Wilmer's question hang between them unanswered. Yes, he had another idea—maybe better, maybe not, but surely safer. After the boys had loaded up and taken off and Lucas had their money in his pocket, the three of them would ride back to Jerry's house in the pickup truck, leaving the boy locked in the equipment room. Lucas was sure that Wilmer and Jerry would buy the idea of putting off dealing with the problem until to-morrow. Then they'd split up the money as usual and he and Wilmer would leave for the motel at Yellville, like they always did. Only this time, they wouldn't go there. They would drive back to the barn, turn the boy loose, and drive away—to Texas or California or wherever. Let Jerry explain things to the sheriff.

"One other thing," Lucas said, as if Wilmer's question had never been asked. "When you talk to Jerry, tell him not to say anything to that wife of his."

"Huh?"

"Didn't you hear me?"

"Yeah, okay."

CHAPTER 10

ROBBIE'S heartbeat was back to normal, no longer pounding so hard that he felt it in his throat. He was breathing evenly now, not taking short, quick gasps. The men had been looking for him. There was no doubt about that. Eric must have told them that his younger brother was lost and asked for their help. Instead, they had grabbed Eric, and then they had come outside to look for him.

But they hadn't found him!

For the first time, Robbie felt hunger pangs. Well, nothing to be done about that. He decided to try not to think about it.

So what now?

Maybe he should sit here all night and then strike out through the woods at dawn. Then he would at least have the sun for a guide and be sure he was going in a straight line and not just wandering in circles. If he kept walking, he was sure to come upon a road or a house or the river—somewhere that people would be able to help him. Besides, if he stayed here all night, he would know if they moved Eric—or if his brother managed to escape. Yes, staying put and then heading out in the morning seemed like a good idea. As a matter of fact, it was his only idea.

The light coming through the cracks between the barn's timbers looked like glowing strings hanging in the darkness. Once, he saw something move along, dulling the glitter of the cracks of light one after another. He guessed that somebody was walking around in the barn.

As he continued to stare at the barn, it occurred to Robbie that he might be able to see through the cracks—maybe he could see Eric.

Half-leaning and half-sitting on the corner of an old wooden table against the wall, Eric surveyed his surroundings in the small equipment room.

A lone bulb at the end of a cord dangling from the ceiling cast a shadowy light around the room. A moth was dive-bombing the bulb.

As soon as Wilmer had shut him in the room, Eric had tried the knob. It turned, but the door didn't give. He pushed harder, again and again, but still it wouldn't budge. It must be bolted on the outside, he concluded.

Eric knew that, even if he got the door open, he'd still have to deal with those two men. But what if he could get out of the room by some other means? There was no window, but the boards that made up the outside wall of the barn were old and half-rotten. He could feel air whistling in through the gaps between them. Maybe he could move a board and slip out that way. . . .

But for all the junk that littered the room, there was nothing that looked useful for breaking through the boards. Sure, there were a few cutting tools—a rusty old crosscut saw, an electric saw that looked like it was missing half its parts—but nothing that looked like it would work both quickly and quietly. What he really needed was a crowbar so that he could pry at the boards.

His gaze passed over and then returned to an open metal toolbox, heavily splotched with rust, resting on the end of the table. Inside was a hand chisel—not very big, not nearly as useful as a crowbar would have been. But it was the closest thing to a prying tool in the room, and it would have to do.

Eric took the chisel and crossed over to the back of the room. He knelt down next to the wall and carefully, quietly, started to push and tug each board, trying to find the loosest, most rotten one.

The boards were arranged vertically. They were about ten inches wide and, judging from a small knothole that went all the way through one of them, about two inches thick. Eric whistled softly in appreciation. He'd helped his grandpa and dad build an addition to the house, and he knew that big slabs of wood like these were pretty expensive. They weren't the kind of boards you'd waste on housing animals nowadays. But just his luck—this old barn had been built in the days when hardwood had been cheap and plentiful, and it was going to be mighty difficult getting one of the pieces to move.

Eric chose a likely-looking board—it was the most warped of the bunch—and jammed the chisel between it and the heavy cross-timber that ran along the floor. The wood was soft with age, and the chisel sank into the seam about a quarter of an inch.

When he pushed against the chisel to separate the board from the beam, however, the chisel tip simply dug a gouge into the cross-timber and popped out.

"Just my luck," Eric muttered to himself in frustration.

He moved the chisel to the left a little and tried again, this time pounding at the head of the chisel with the heel of his hand. If he had been able to make noise, he would have hammered at the chisel with something. But hammering sounds would surely bring the men into the room.

The knuckles of his right hand scraped against the board as he pounded at the chisel. The sting increased with each blow.

Twenty-one, twenty-two . . .

He stopped. The chisel had sunk about two inches into the seam between board and beam.

He pushed with both hands, putting all the weight he could muster against the chisel. If the chisel was in deep enough, if it had enough leverage, maybe he could pop the board away from the cross-timber. And then slip out through—

The chisel snapped out of the beam, cracking his raw knuckles against the board with a loud slap. He stifled a cry of pain.

He'd dug a two-inch chunk of wood out of the beam. But the beam was eight inches wide at least. He'd have to dig away at a lot more of it before the board would come free.

Outside, Robbie heard the slap. He jumped to his feet and watched the barn. A shadow moved across the streaks of light shining through the gaps in the planking, going toward the back of the building.

That was where the noise had come from—the back of the barn.

Then he heard a voice but couldn't make out the words.

The door to the equipment room flew open and Lucas stepped in. "What's going on?" he asked.

Wilmer was behind him, peering into the room.

"I was, uh, sitting on the table, and I knocked something off." Eric motioned at the chisel, now lying in the middle of the floor.

Wilmer went to pick up the chisel. As he was stooping over, he said, "Hey, Lucas, look at that. Looks like something's been chewing at the wood here." He stood and faced his brother. "Must be a rat."

"It was a rat all right," Lucas said, snatching the chisel from Wilmer. He held the tool under Eric's nose and said, "We've got some friends coming here in a little while. If you make a single sound, I'm going to hurt you real bad. Understand?"

Eric met Lucas's eyes and nodded slowly. His mind raced, trying to weigh the significance of visitors. Why didn't this man want his friends to know Eric was here? Maybe they wouldn't like the idea of this man holding him prisoner. Maybe they would insist that he let Eric go.

But then what? How was he going to find Robbie?

He couldn't shout without alerting the men. And he couldn't see in the darkness. He was sure that his younger brother, wherever he might be, was frightened—alone in the woods and lost in the black of night. Even if somehow Robbie had made his way back to their camp on the river, by now he would know that Eric was missing.

Eric took a breath. Before he could begin to help Robbie, he had to help himself. He had to escape!

Lucas grinned at Eric. Then, as if he had read Eric's mind, he said, "These men won't be of a mind to help you, if that's what you're thinking. They'd want to hurt you even more than I would."

Eric gave a little nod.

Lucas turned and shoved past Wilmer, leaving the room.

As Wilmer closed the door, he said, "We ought to do something with him now, before the boys get here. We've got time."

"Shut up," Lucas said. "I know what I'm doing."

Wilmer's words—"do something with him"—sent a shiver through Eric.

Robbie watched the shadows move back across the barn, from the rear to the front.

In the few moments that followed, nothing moved inside as far as Robbie could tell.

He took a couple of steps forward, then stopped. His heart was pounding. He listened. There was nothing—no more racket from the back of the barn, no scraping sound of someone opening the barn door, not even the muffled sound of voices. He looked to his left, in the direction in which the red-haired man had driven off in the pickup truck. If the man came back while he was near the barn, Robbie would be caught in the headlights. He squinted into the darkness. There were no headlights in sight. There was no sound of the pickup truck approaching.

Robbie walked slowly, carefully, down the slope and across the open area to the barn.

He peered through one of the cracks. There they were, the other two men, seated at a table, drinking out of coffee cups.

He did not see Eric in the narrow slice of the barn he could see through the crack.

He looked back to his left—still no headlights in sight—and then carefully edged to his right, toward the rear of the barn.

Starting about halfway along the length of the barn, the ground sloped down. Half the barn stood on a crumbling stone foundation that, at its highest, at the very rear of the structure, was a good ten feet.

Robbie crept down the slope until he rounded the corner of the barn. He stood directly below the part of the barn where he believed Eric was being held.

Robbie thought about calling up to his brother but decided against it. From where he stood, Eric was high above him, on the other side of a wall. He'd have to call pretty loudly, and risk alerting the men inside too.

He reached out and tested the foundation. A stone, along with a chunk of powdery mortar, came off into his hand. He'd never be able to climb such a crumbly wall without making a racket and possibly falling and injuring himself.

How could he let Eric know he was there without giving himself away to the men in the barn?

Robbie stood in the barnyard and thought hard. And then an idea came to him.

Eric scanned the room. Lucas had taken the chisel, and there was nothing else Eric could use to pry at the boards. He sat heavily on the table and sighed. This was quite a mess he'd gotten himself into.

Whoot, whoot! Eric's thoughts were interrupted by the loud hooting of an owl. It sounded awfully close by.

Whoot, whoot!

The owl hooted again. Or was it an owl? Eric had spent a lot of nights in the woods, and he'd never heard an owl that sounded like that. It was more like someone doing a bad imitation of an owl.

Robbie!

Whoot, whoooot!

The "owl" sounded more insistent this time. What did Robbie want? What did he expect Eric to do, hoot back at him? What good would that do? They couldn't communicate by hooting.

Whoot, whoot!

He keeps hooting twice, Eric thought, as if that's supposed to mean something. . . . Wait a second—the code! Robbie was using the code he'd made up their first day on the river.

Eric had to hand it to his brother. He might be a pain sometimes, but he was resourceful when the chips were down.

Now how did that code go? Two taps—or hoots, in this case—meant . . . Eric racked his brain. He wished he'd taken Robbie more seriously before.

Two taps . . . "What's the matter?" Yeah, that was it. Robbie was trying to ask him what was going on.

Now, what was the rest of it? Eric cast his mind back, picturing himself and Robbie on the riverbank, eating lunch, Robbie tapping away at his aluminum cup. Three taps . . . "I'm hurt."

That didn't do him any good. What was the last one?

Eric smiled as the last bit of code came back to him: Two quick taps, then a pause followed by a third tap meant "Get help fast."

Eric hopped off the table and started to hoot in reply, then stopped himself. Lucas and Wilmer were right outside his door. Even if they didn't recognize Robbie's hooting as not being a real owl, they'd surely get suspicious if it sounded like there was an owl right there in the barn. He'd have to signal Robbie in some other way—preferably silently.

He looked around the room. On the table, a bunch of loose bolts and screws lay scattered in the top of a cardboard produce box. He glanced up to the single lightbulb hanging on a cord from the ceiling. That's it, thought Eric.

Quietly, he scooped the bolts and screws out of the box top and placed them on the table. Then he took the box top and walked beneath the lightbulb. By placing the cardboard in front of the bulb, he could blot out the light shining in Robbie's direction. Eric was sure there were enough knotholes and cracks between the boards for Robbie to catch on to what he was doing.

He raised the cardboard in front of the bulb once, twice; he paused, then raised it once more: "*Get help fast.*"

He waited. Silence. No hooting.

He sent the code again. Once, twice, pause, a third time.

Silence. Then a long, low, mournful *Whooooo*.

It wasn't part of the code, but Eric was pretty

sure he knew what Robbie was saying: "Message received."

Just to make sure, though, and to impress upon Robbie that he really meant it, Eric sent the code one more time.

This time Robbie called back, *Who, who, who, who, who—whooot!*

Eric frowned. What was that supposed to mean?

Then it occurred to him: There had been one more line of code, one that Eric had made up himself. Robbie had gotten Eric's message the first time all right, and he didn't appreciate being told again. So he was using Eric's own contribution to the code: "Five quick knocks on the head mean . . ."

Eric grinned. He knew exactly what Robbie was saying to him: "I am an eleven-year-old doofus— *not!*"

CHAPTER 11

"**Y**OU never listen to me, Lucas, but I'm telling you we'd better do something with that boy."

"Don't worry about it."

"He's going to shout or kick up a ruckus or something while the boys are here, sure as the world's round."

Lucas leered at Wilmer. "How do you know the world's round?" he asked.

"Huh? What do you mean? Everybody knows the world is round."

"Sometimes I wonder about you, Wilmer."

Wilmer leaned forward, ignoring Lucas's remark, and said, "The least we ought to do is gag and tie him."

"Do you think that would keep him from grunting or kicking, if he had a mind to call attention to himself?"

Wilmer frowned while he weighed the question. Then he said, "We could gag and tie him—and take him out in the woods a ways and dump him until the boys have come and gone. That way, he could grunt and kick all he wanted, and nobody'd notice. We could go get him later. He won't be going no place if I hog-tie him." Wilmer smiled, satisfied with his logic.

Lucas forced himself to think that one over. The idea made sense. But accepting a suggestion from Wilmer didn't come easy for him. It was bad enough that his brother was the one who had found Jerry and his barn. Wilmer was forever reminding him of it. That was the way it always was when Lucas took up one of Wilmer's ideas. Wilmer made a nuisance of himself, always reminding him where the idea had come from.

In the end, it was the smile on Wilmer's face that made up Lucas's mind. "Naw," he said. "Forget it."

Wilmer's grin faded a little. "Why?"

Lucas leaned toward Wilmer, his mouth a straight line. He said, "Wilmer, there's one thing you didn't remember."

"What's that?"

"Little brother is out there somewhere. If he stumbles on big brother, or hears him grunting and moving around, do you know what we've got?" When

Wilmer didn't speak immediately, Lucas continued. "We've got big brother loose in the woods, running for help. You didn't think of that, did you?"

"The little kid's not out there. We went and looked."

"My way is better, Wilmer, and you don't need to bother your head with it."

Wilmer's smile was completely gone. "You're not going to be saying that when he hollers while the boys are here."

Lucas took a sip of his coffee and looked at Wilmer. He figured that he had a lot of other things to think about, but if Wilmer was going to keep yammering, he might as well stop trying to think and explain what was going on.

"He's not going to holler, Wilmer, because he doesn't want to holler."

"Why not?"

"You heard me tell him that we've got some men coming here, and that if he made the slightest little bitty sound, I was going to hurt him a lot. Don't you think he understood that?"

"I guess."

"And that the men coming here would want to hurt him even more than I would, if they knew he was here. He understood that too, don't you think?"

"Okay."

"I persuaded him not to make any noise—and that's better than all the gagging and tying in the world."

"Oh." Wilmer looked puzzled; then he smiled. "I see." He paused. "Lucas, you already had this all worked out, didn't you?"

"Don't I always?"

CHAPTER 12

ROBBIE walked carefully away from the barn and toward the woods, glancing to his right twice to see if headlights were approaching. There were none—the red-haired man in the pickup truck wasn't on his way back yet.

A few steps into the woods, he stopped and looked back at the barn, seeing nothing but the streaks of light coming through the cracks.

He looked at the sky, at the sliver of a moon and the black blanket dotted with stars. Eric had signaled to him to go get help, but how was he supposed to find it out here in the middle of nowhere? He could stumble around in the dark woods, looking for a house or a road, all night and not find anything—and by morning, it might be too late.

With a feeling of dread, Robbie realized that his only chance was to follow the road the pickup truck had taken. He didn't like having to risk being spotted by the red-haired man or one of his friends. But how else was he going to find a main road?

He had no idea how deep into the woods the barn was. But how far could it be to a main road? A couple of miles? Even five? In the daytime, he could run five miles in an hour, easy. But at night, having to walk carefully so as not to trip over anything in the dark, it'd take much longer, possibly hours. Did Eric have that kind of time? Robbie didn't know, but in any case, he had no other options.

With a last glance at the barn, Robbie set off along the dirt road. It was pitted and rough, and tree limbs and bushes drooped into the path. He stumbled down a sudden sharp slope in the road, grabbing at a branch to steady himself. At the bottom, he looked around in the darkness. Maybe his eyes had adjusted to the darkness, as his father had once explained to him, but it wasn't helping much. He began to climb the opposite slope.

At the top, he sensed, rather than saw, a flatness in the road ahead of him.

He wanted to run, or at least jog, but thought better of it. He wasn't able to see the ground where he was stepping. He tripped over a small fallen tree at one point and almost fell. Then his foot came down on the side of a rock, and he stumbled. The twisting feeling in his ankle reminded him of his father's broken ankle and also of the time Eric had sprained an ankle playing football. For a long time, his brother had had to walk with crutches. No, running was out of the question. He might sprain an ankle or trip and fall or run into a tree. . . .

Robbie walked along, his right hand raised in front of him, shoving aside the occasional small branch and feeling his way around trees.

Everything seemed to be a hillside, going up or going down. Walking up was easier than walking down, he decided.

For a time, he counted his steps. He didn't know why. He just did it.

He stopped counting when he noticed headlights blinking and bobbing, coming toward him.

He dived into the underbrush at the side of the road and crawled another twenty feet into the woods. He got behind a large tree trunk and sat up, pressing his back against the rough bark. Hoping that the driver behind those headlights hadn't seen him, he closed his eyes and tried to slow his breathing. He could feel his pulse beating in his temples.

As the lights approached, Robbie could tell that there was more than one set of headlights. He peeked around the tree as the first vehicle passed. It was the pickup the red-haired man had driven away. It did not stop or even slow down. The man must not have seen him. Then three more vehicles drove by—a largish truck and two cars.

After the taillights of the last car vanished, Robbie crawled out from behind the tree and made his way back to the dirt road. He looked in the direction the vehicles were headed—toward the barn. The drone of their engines faded as they got farther away.

Satisfied that they would not be coming back anytime soon, Robbie turned and started down the road again, toward help.

Eric leaned against the table, suddenly realizing he was tired. It was late by now, and he'd risen at dawn and spent the whole day paddling the canoe.

He had given up on the idea of prying away one of the boards. They were just too strong, and besides, he had no tools to work with.

His only hope was Robbie.

How long had his little brother been gone? He wasn't sure. In one way, it seemed only a moment ago that he had signaled to Robbie to get help. In another way, it seemed his kid brother had been gone forever.

What if Robbie failed to return with help before the men decided the time had come to dispose of him?

That word—*dispose*—put a frown on Eric's face. What would they do with him? A couple of men in a car-theft ring wouldn't commit murder to protect the secrecy of their chop shop—would they?

CHAPTER 13

THROUGH a crack between the boards, Lucas saw a flash of light in the darkness outside, then another. Then he heard the sounds of the approaching vehicles.

"Hey, they're here," Wilmer said.

"Open the door for them," Lucas told his brother, "and tell Jerry to leave the pickup outside for the time being."

"Right." Wilmer moved toward the door.

"And while you've got him alone out there, tell him about our little problem."

Wilmer looked back as he swung the door open. "Okay."

Lucas wondered about the wisdom of having Wilmer brief Jerry. Jerry was almost as dumb as Wilmer, and if Wilmer didn't mess up the telling, there was a good chance Jerry would mess up trying to grasp what was going on. But, Lucas figured, he had no choice. He was the one who always told the boys where to park the cars in the barn, and where to back up the truck. If he left that to Wilmer and instead went out to talk to Jerry alone, the boys were certain to notice and figure something was wrong. They were a suspicious bunch anyway.

Lucas stepped into the wide doorway and waved.

Wilmer was over next to the pickup truck, saying something to Jerry, and then, when Jerry steered the pickup around the side of the barn, he followed him. At least Wilmer got that much of it right.

The car behind the pickup truck—a blue Buick Le Sabre—nosed into the doorway as Lucas moved to the side.

The window on the driver's side whirred down. "How you doing, Lucas?"

"Just fine, Jake."

"This little baby's got everything on it you can think of, except a TV set."

Lucas grinned. "Good," he said. "Pull it on over there, all the way up to the back wall."

The car moved past slowly and a second car—a Chrysler Imperial—rolled into the doorway.

Again, a window whirred down. "Lucas, you look as mean as ever."

"I am. Good to see you, Henry. Pull it in right behind Jake."

As the car rolled past, Lucas turned his attention to the last vehicle, a six-wheel truck. It was the same one they always used—small enough to follow Jerry through the trees and around the rocks to the barn, big and strong enough to carry a huge load out.

Lucas made a little twirling motion with his right hand, indicating that the driver should turn around and back into the barn. It annoyed him that he always had to give this direction. The same driver, a kid named Johnny, was at the wheel every time, but it seemed he couldn't remember from one trip to the next that he had to back the truck into the barn for loading.

Johnny pulled around to the side of the barn, not far from where Wilmer and Jerry were talking. That wasn't good. Lucas walked to the corner of the barn, heard the trucker call out a greeting to Wilmer, saw Wilmer wave in response, and then watched as the trucker backed his rig around and into the barn. It was okay.

"Have you got another cup of that coffee?"

It was Jake.

"Sure," Lucas said, and led him to a cabinet at the back of the barn. "Henry, do you want a cup of coffee?"

"Yeah."

Johnny was approaching. "I could use one too."

Lucas had passed out cups and the four of them

were walking toward the coffeepot on the table when Wilmer and Jerry appeared in the doorway alongside the six-wheeler.

The sight of the two of them stopped Lucas in his tracks for a moment. Jerry, who grinned even when he was worrying, wasn't grinning now. He looked as if he had seen a ghost, and all the blood had rushed out of his face. Wilmer clearly was puzzled, wearing the expression of a man who knows something has gone wrong but can't figure out what.

Lucas recovered quickly and called out, "Do you two want coffee?"

Jerry shook his head.

Wilmer said, "Nah, I don't need any more."

The three drivers filled their cups and took seats at the long table, obviously in no hurry to get on with the loading and be on their way.

Lucas sat down with them. This wasn't the time to try to rush them. They were entitled to a cup of coffee after several hours behind the steering wheel, and they knew it. But there was something Lucas could do to move things along. "Wilmer," he said, "you and Jerry start moving some of that stuff. Get it over behind the truck so we can start loading."

"What's the matter with Jerry?" Jake asked in a low voice. He was climbing out of the back of the truck after putting down a stack of car radios. Jerry was at the other side of the barn, picking up a load.

"What do you mean?" Lucas was standing at the open end of the truck with a clipboard in his hand, counting items going in and jotting them down.

"He's usually a grinning fool, the friendliest guy in the world. But since we got here, he looks like he lost his best friend."

Lucas glanced at Jerry, then turned back to Jake. It was obvious that something was bothering him. "You don't know his wife," Lucas said, thinking fast.

"Nah."

"She's one tough woman. Gives him a hard time sometimes. He's been having some trouble at home. That's all." He looked again at Jerry. "I'll talk to him. Maybe he ought to go on home, and Wilmer and I can catch a ride back to town with you."

When Jake moved on and Wilmer approached, Lucas handed him the clipboard and pencil and said, "Here, you count the stuff for a minute. I've got to talk to Jerry."

"He's okay. Just scared."

"Do what I tell you—and for once, get it right. And quit looking at the equipment room like you think it's going to explode any minute."

Wilmer took the clipboard and pencil, and Lucas walked away before he could answer.

"Jerry, let's go outside where we can talk."

Jerry nodded. "Yeah, I need to talk to you."

As they walked across the barn toward the doorway, Lucas saw Jake speaking to Henry. Undoubtedly, he was telling him about Jerry's marital problems. Lucas hoped that none of them would ask Wilmer any questions. There wasn't any guessing what his brother might say. Lucas figured he'd better not waste any more time with Jerry than he could help.

They were barely around the corner of the barn when Jerry, his voice quivering, said, "Lucas, you ain't gonna kill him, are you?"

"Naw, of course not."

"But Wilmer said—"

"Jerry, you know that Wilmer hasn't got any sense."

"I just don't want no murder in my barn."

"There's not going to be any murder in your barn. Just cool down. Everything is going to be all right."

"Then what are we going to do?"

"We'll work it out. I've got a plan. But we can't do anything until we get the boys loaded up and out of here. Don't you see?"

"I guess." Jerry stood there, not moving, for a moment. Then he said, almost to himself, "Dorothy is going to have a fit."

"Then don't tell her."

"She said at the start that I shouldn't get mixed up in this."

"She likes the money, doesn't she?"

"I guess."

"Then let's just leave it at that."

CHAPTER 14

ERIC stood with his ear to the door.

He had heard the sounds of cars being pulled into the barn, then of doors being slammed. He heard a heavy truck rumble up to the barn and stop. He heard men talking about coffee, and then some mumbled conversation.

Now it sounded as if they were going back and forth, probably carrying car parts to the truck. He heard them calling out to one another from time to time.

He couldn't be sure, but it sounded as if there were at least three new men. Possibly four.

When everything was loaded, Eric figured, the new men would probably be leaving. Then he was going to be left with Lucas and Wilmer. Plus that third guy he'd seen them with back at the river, most likely.

That was when something was going to happen—unless Eric made something happen earlier.

He could shout and kick the door to let the new men know he was there. But Lucas had warned him not to make a sound, because these men would hurt him even worse than Lucas would. Maybe Lucas was lying, because he knew these men wouldn't want to be involved in anything more serious than stolen cars and they would insist on releasing Eric unharmed. But then, maybe Lucas had told him the truth.

Eric decided to take his chances waiting—waiting for Robbie to return with help.

Robbie walked along the dirt road as quickly as he dared. Every minute that passed made him more nervous. He didn't know what all those cars driving toward the barn might mean, but he had a feeling they weren't good news for Eric.

Robbie squinted into the darkness ahead of him. Nothing but more dirt road and trees, as far as he could tell. When would this trail come to a real road, with pavement and traffic, and people who could help him?

Normally, he wasn't afraid of the dark—that was for babies. Plenty of times, he'd stayed out playing catch with his friends until they could barely see the ball. Then they'd quit—game called on account of darkness—and he'd jog home, passing from one streetlight to the next. And he'd never been scared, not once.

But a strange, unknown forest at night was different from the familiar streets of home.

He picked up his pace, half-jogging as his anxiety rose.

Suddenly, he froze. He'd heard—or thought he'd heard, anyway—a rustling in the brush to his left. He wondered what could have made the sound—some kind of wild animal? A wolf, or maybe a bear? Standing stock-still in the middle of the road, Robbie felt exposed, vulnerable, and very much alone—more alone than he'd ever felt in his life.

He wondered briefly if this was how the early settlers had felt, the trappers and mountain men who'd first entered the wild country. In school, he'd read about Lewis and Clark. Had they too felt alone and afraid at times? Probably they had.

The thought of grown men, tough men who'd tamed a wilderness, feeling the same things he felt cheered Robbie a little. He was still afraid, but he no longer felt so alone.

The bushes rustled again, and this time he knew it wasn't his imagination.

Well, he could run. But if it was a wolf or a bear, it would be able to catch him from behind. Better to stay where he was and face whatever was making those noises.

The brush rustled again. Robbie was setting himself in a crouch, bracing for the animal to pounce, when a fat raccoon waddled into the road, followed by three babies.

The mother raccoon looked at Robbie and blinked unconcernedly, then shuffled across the road and into the brush on the other side. Her babies scampered after her.

Robbie blew a sigh of relief, then burst out laughing.

There was no wolf or bear, no danger at all! Just a chubby raccoon family out for a stroll.

As he started up the road again, he realized he wasn't afraid anymore. He'd been ready to stand up to danger. So what if the wolf had turned out to be a raccoon? He'd met his fears face-to-face, and he hadn't run. Now he was sure he'd get to the road in time to save his brother.

Soon he found himself climbing a small rise and entering a clearing. The starry sky opened up on either side of him as the trees dropped away, and he felt smooth blacktop under his sneakers. He looked around and saw yellow lane-divider lines receding into the distance to the left and right.

Yes! A highway!

But where were the cars?

He had expected to see headlights of cars and trucks moving along the highway, and maybe hear traffic, long before he walked out of the woods. But there had been only darkness and night sounds all around. And now there was still nothing but darkness.

He stood on the blacktop and looked down the road in both directions. Nothing. He wanted to shout in frustration. Surely someone would come along. But when? He needed them now—right now! His shoulders sagged a little. There was nothing to do but wait.

Then he looked back to his left. There was a flicker of light through the trees. Maybe a car was approaching around the curve. He turned.

The headlights shined on the trees before the car appeared from around the curve. Then there was a set of headlights approaching him.

Robbie stood at the edge of the road and began waving both hands above his head.

CHAPTER 15

LUCAS took a look inside the truck—less than half-full—and walked across to the table where everyone was seated, talking and drinking coffee. A rest break, the boys had said. They had arrived earlier than usual and now, with the extra time, they weren't in any hurry to load up and move out. "If we get back too early," Johnny had explained, "we'll just have to wait for somebody to show up before we can unload."

Lucas poured himself a cup of coffee and sat down with them. There was nothing else to do. If he pushed too hard, they might get suspicious that something was wrong somewhere. They were already wondering why Jerry looked as if he was attending his best friend's funeral.

Maybe he should have gone ahead and sent Jerry back to his house, gotten him out of here. But no, there was nothing but trouble sure to come out of sending Jerry home. Dorothy would have noticed that he was worrying and would have gotten the whole story out of him in no time flat. And being smarter than her husband, she probably would have called the cops herself, trying to get a better deal for the two of them. No, it was better to have Jerry stay right where he was.

Jake looked across at Lucas. "When'll you have these two new ones ready?" he asked.

"Can't say."

"They'll be asking, you know."

"You're not going to be coming back for the stuff off just two cars, are you?"

"Never can tell. They've got a lot of expensive equipment on them. Not like selling mufflers, you know."

Lucas nodded. "I'll give you a call, like always."

"Are you getting nervous, Lucas?"

Lucas eyed Jake evenly without blinking. "I never get nervous. But I've got sense enough to know that all this activity—lights, a big truck pulling in—might attract some attention."

Jake laughed. "Out here in the woods?"

Lucas didn't smile. "You've seen them houses out there on the highway, haven't you? They got people living in them. Those folks go outside sometimes, and they look out their windows sometimes."

"There's none around where we pull off the highway."

Lucas nodded. "And there's always the risk of somebody stumbling onto us."

"We can handle that, if it happens."

Without thinking, Lucas glanced at the door to the equipment room. Catching himself, he turned back to Jake and said casually, "It's just better if it doesn't happen at all. Are you boys ready to get back to work?"

"Okay, okay," Jake said.

They got to their feet and ambled toward a pile of equipment stacked against the wall.

"C'mon, Wilmer," Lucas said. "You and Jerry help them. We've got to get this wrapped up."

They were almost finished.

Lucas stood at the rear of the truck, counting the items as they were brought over and jotting down model names and numbers.

Wilmer, leaning in, said, "Maybe I'd better go check on him."

"No."

"We haven't heard anything in a long time."

"That's what I told him to do—stay quiet."

"Maybe he got away."

Henry was approaching.

"No. Go on, get back to work."

"What's up?" Henry asked.

"Wilmer's lazy, that's all."

Henry laughed. "That ain't nothing new."

With a soft popping sound—*pfft!*—the lightbulb dangling from the cord above Eric went out.

The darkness wasn't total. The lights from the rest of the barn shone through the cracks in the wall in tiny fragments.

But the sudden darkness frightened him. Maybe somebody in the barn would notice that the light had gone out. Lucas or Wilmer might think he was up to something. Or one of the other men might notice the change and come to investigate. From the last bit of conversation he had heard through the door, Eric was glad the new arrivals did not know he was there. He wanted to keep it that way.

Eric stepped away from the door and his foot bumped something, and then something fell to the floor with a metallic clanging sound. In the quiet of the equipment room, the sound rang out like a fire bell.

Eric's heart leaped into his throat, and he froze where he stood.

He heard someone say, "What was that?"

Then, quickly, Lucas was speaking loudly: "Must

be that possum again. Wilmer, you get in there and check on it."

"Me?" Wilmer's voice was an octave higher than normal.

"I'll do it," somebody said.

Lucas spoke again: "No, Henry, Wilmer can check it. You keep loading. I want to get this job done."

Eric heard the door bolt slide. He saw the door open a couple of inches, letting in a stream of light. He heard Wilmer say to himself, "It's dark." Then he watched as the man stepped back out of the doorway, letting the door swing slowly shut. Eric heard Wilmer say to someone, probably Lucas, "The light's burned out. I need the flashlight."

In a few moments, the door opened again and Wilmer entered behind the beam of a large flashlight. He did not speak. He shined the beam in Eric's face and said, "Uh-huh" as he confirmed that Eric was still in the room. "Don't make no more noise," he whispered. "Lucas said so."

Eric nodded.

Wilmer opened the door and stepped back out, closing it and sliding the bolt home again.

Eric heard him say, "It must've been that possum, but he's gone now."

CHAPTER 16

THE headlights drew near—and then passed Robbie by.

It was a pickup truck, and it looked old. Robbie turned and watched the taillights moving away from him.

He was sure the driver had seen him. The bright beam of the headlights had hit him, making him squint, and the driver had veered a little to go around him.

Couldn't the driver see that he needed help?

Then the truck slowed, stopped, and began backing up.

Robbie ran along the shoulder of the road, toward the truck.

Suddenly, a fear struck him. His parents had told him all his life never to accept a ride from a stranger. They never really explained what the danger might be, but Robbie had gotten the message that something terrible might happen if he ever got into a car with someone he didn't know.

But by now he was alongside the truck, looking up at the face of a woman in the passenger seat. Beyond her, there was a man leaning forward over the steering wheel, looking at him.

Robbie sat in the cab of the pickup truck, now parked on the shoulder of the road. He was next to the window. The man at the wheel and the woman between them had listened without speaking while Robbie blurted out his story.

When he had finished, the man, staring straight ahead through the windshield into the darkness, said, "It sounds like that old barn of Jerry Coleman's."

The woman said, "Jerry would never be mixed up in anything like this."

"Umm. Maybe not. But it sure sounds like his barn is mixed up in something."

"We've got to hurry," Robbie said.

"Yes." The man leaned toward the dashboard, turned on a citizens band radio, and lifted the microphone. "Happy Cherokee calling Cousin Smokey. Are you there?"

"This is Cousin Smokey."

"Harvey, this is Gene Worth. I'm about three or four miles south of the Buffalo on Highway Fourteen, just short of the Morton's place, and I need help."

"What's the matter?"

"I can't say."

There was a long pause. Then the man said, "How much help do you need?"

"Probably a lot."

"I'll be right there."

"Better come prepared. I mean it."

"I understand."

"Over and out."

The man replaced the microphone. "Deputy sheriff," he said to Robbie. "I'm a police officer myself." Then he smiled and added, "This *was* my day off." The smile faded and he asked, "Do they have a CB radio in that barn?"

"I don't know."

"Well, if they heard me, maybe they'll think it's a man with a flat tire."

In the cab of the pickup truck, the minutes ticked by silently as Robbie stared straight ahead. Where were the police? Why didn't they hurry? Then two sheriff's cars glided to a halt on the shoulder behind the pickup, and at almost the same moment, a state police car pulled up from the other direction.

The officers, four of them in all, walked toward the truck.

Gene Worth said, "C'mon, Robbie," and opened his door.

Robbie opened the door on his side and tumbled out, then ran around to the back of the pickup truck to join the group.

He stood and listened while Gene Worth briefed the other officers, repeating Robbie's story. The men glanced at Robbie from time to time. They seemed to be having trouble believing the story.

A pickup truck heading north passed them, slowing down but not stopping.

"I figure," Worth said at the finish, "that it's probably Jerry Coleman's old barn."

One of the officers said to Robbie, "Son, this is all true, isn't it?"

Robbie blinked. "Yes, sir. I swear it."

The man nodded. "Okay."

Another officer asked, "Are these men armed?"

Robbie shook his head. "I don't know."

The first officer said, "We'll have to assume they're armed."

"Yeah," another said, "and that there are five or six of them. We're going to need help."

"Maybe we'd do better to wait until daylight."

Robbie felt his heart skip a beat. "No!" he said. "My brother—"

"He's right," Gene Worth said. "That boy they're holding is in danger."

Robbie glanced up at the word *danger*. Yes, Eric was in danger. He'd said so himself, in code: "Get help fast." But hearing the word spoken by an adult, to a police officer . . . it gave Robbie a shiver.

"Gene, can you lead us to that barn in the dark?"

"I think so. There's no real road—it's more like a wide path, really—but it's not far. And if the lights are on in the barn, it ought to be pretty easy to spot from a distance."

The officer nodded. "Okay. Let's get some help, and we'll go in. On foot, okay?"

Everyone in the circle nodded.

Lucas swung the big rear door of the truck closed and threw the latch. Finally they were finished. These guys moved even slower than Wilmer.

With the clipboard in his hand, he turned and walked toward the table to add up the cost of the shipment.

Everybody else but Jake was already seated on benches at the table. Jake was pouring himself a cup of coffee. Well, thought Lucas, he'd better drink it quick. I'm going to add this up, get the money in my pocket, and get them out of here. And then get myself out.

He glanced at Jerry, sitting there all hunched over, seeming to shrink with every passing minute.

Yeah, Jerry knew he had a problem. Everybody else

could scatter. But not Jerry. The three delivery men, relieved of their money and with their load on board, would be gone, never even knowing the boy had been in the equipment room. Lucas himself, with Wilmer, would vanish without a trace. Lucas was thinking they might go to Texas. But Jerry couldn't leave, couldn't vanish. It was his barn. He lived in Gilbert. Jerry was the one who was going to be stuck with a collection of fenders and bumpers, stacks of used tires, and two stolen cars, all of which he wouldn't be able to explain.

Watching him sitting there, Lucas reflected that Jerry did not know just how bad his problem really was. Once the boys were on their way and Lucas had the money in his pocket, he and Wilmer would ride back to Jerry's house with him to pick up their car, as usual. Then he and Wilmer would come back to the barn and turn the boy loose. That done, they were going to put as many miles as possible between themselves and the barn before daylight. It was the only smart thing to do. Sure, it meant the end of the moneymaking deal they had here. But they could get another operation going someplace else. Too bad about Jerry, though, being left holding the bag.

Lucas dropped the clipboard on the table, pulled a small calculator out of his shirt pocket, and sat down. From the bottom of the sheaves of paper on the clipboard, he extracted a worn page with a penciled list of items and prices—the negotiated amounts he, Wilmer, and Jerry received for everything they salvaged from stolen cars.

Jake walked over with his coffee and sat down. "You know," he said, "I'm going to come down here and float this river sometime. It's pretty around here, and I'll bet there're lots of bass in that river."

Johnny laughed. "What do you mean, 'pretty around here'? You never seen this place in the daylight."

"I can tell. Right, Jerry?"

Lucas, moving a finger over the paper as he punched in the figures and added and multiplied, stopped and looked up.

Jerry brought his head up and looked around. The sound of his name had obviously cut through his thoughts. He looked around. Everyone was watching him. "Huh?" he asked.

"I said it's pretty around here, and there're lots of bass in that river, right?"

Lucas frowned at Jake. He'd seen his kind before, plenty of times. At the first sign of someone looking troubled or weak, they went for the person like a big dog going after raw meat. "Lay off him," Lucas said.

"I just asked him a question."

Jerry mumbled, "Uh-huh."

"Is something wrong with you?" Jake asked.

"No," Jerry said.

Lucas watched Jerry. Why couldn't he pull himself together, just for a few minutes?

Jake, grinning at Jerry's discomfort, wasn't finished. He said, "Lucas, what's wrong with Jerry?"

"I told you—he's got some problems at home."

"Oh, yeah," Jake said, satisfied that he had forced Lucas to mention Jerry's problem in front of Jerry and everyone else.

"What's that?" Jerry said.

"Forget it," Lucas snapped. "Shut up, and let me finish this."

Lucas returned his attention to the clipboard, then announced, "I figure it comes to four thousand two hundred and eighty-five dollars." He grinned at Jake. "Let's make it an even forty-three hundred dollars to cover all that coffee you drank."

"Sounds a little high to me, Lucas."

Lucas glared at Jake for a moment. Then he said, "Are you calling me a liar?"

Jake stared back for a moment, and then he gave Lucas a cold smile. "Naw, of course not. It just sounds like you might've made a mistake."

"Do you want to recount everything?"

"You know we don't have time to take everything out of there and count it. Let's make it thirty-five hundred, and we've got a deal."

"Four thousand."

Jake took a sip of his coffee. "Okay, four thousand."

Lucas grinned. They went through the same routine every time. Lucas cheated, and Jake knew it. But it didn't matter enough to Jake to count along with him. It was easier to haggle at the end. Lucas figured that Jake was probably cheating his receivers, telling them he paid more than he did. Well, that was okay. Everybody made a little money.

Jake took a wallet out of his hip pocket. A small chain connected it to a belt loop on his jeans. He opened the wallet and pulled out a stack of bills. One by one, with a bit of a flourish, he counted out ten one-hundred-dollar bills in a stack on the table.

Lucas counted along with him, keeping his eyes on the green bills.

"Ten," Jake said.

"Yeah, ten."

Jake started counting out a second stack, and Lucas, with some effort, kept his eyes on the bills. This was the stage of the operation—all that money being flashed around, with everyone watching—that always frightened him a little. If Jake or one of the others pulled a gun, they could leave with the shipment in the truck and the money in their pockets. Lucas wouldn't be able even to protest. He didn't want to get shot. He certainly couldn't complain to the police that he'd been robbed. And he didn't have the slightest idea who Jake's bosses were.

Jake finished the second stack and looked up.

Lucas nodded and Jake resumed counting.

At the finish, Lucas picked up the money, folded it, and put it in his pants pocket. "Nice doing business with you," he said.

Jake opened his mouth to speak, but the words they heard in the barn came from somewhere else.

A voice speaking through a bullhorn from outside in the night filled the barn with a sound that made the air seem to vibrate: "This is the police. You are surrounded. Come out with your hands up."

CHAPTER 17

ROBBIE sat in the pickup truck next to Gene Worth's wife, but his thoughts were back at the barn. He wanted to know what was happening—it had been a little while. The pickup was parked on the shoulder of the road. The only light visible was the faint yellowish blur cast ahead of them by the truck's parking lights, and the occasional headlights of a passing car.

The police officers had pulled their cars down the road and off into the woods, to avoid attracting the attention of passersby.

Before leaving, the officers had asked Robbie about Eric's situation. Where was he being held? Was he tied up? Had he been hurt? Was he being watched?

Robbie had answered as best he could, based on what he'd been able to see between the planks in the barn wall. He didn't think Eric was hurt, since his brother hadn't flashed the "I'm hurt" code. He didn't know whether Eric was tied up. He was in a back corner of the barn, in what seemed to be a small separate room. Nobody had been in the room with him, at least not when Robbie had left him there.

Now Robbie worried that maybe the men had moved Eric to another place in the barn. Maybe he would be somewhere else when the officers arrived— somewhere where he might get hurt. Or maybe now there was someone in the room with Eric, watching him.

His thoughts were interrupted when one of the passing cars stopped, backed up, and a man called out, "Myrna, is that you?"

Mrs. Worth, seated behind the wheel, leaned out the window and said, "Hi, Jeff. Yes, it's me."

"Is anything wrong?"

"No, nothing's wrong. Gene will be back in a minute."

"Are you sure?"

"Yes, sure."

After a moment, he asked, "Is that someone in the truck with you?"

"Yes, a little boy who got lost when he wandered away from his campsite. Gene has gone to find his older brother."

"Does he need help?"

"No. Everything's all right."

After another pause, the man called out, "Okay," and drove away.

Robbie looked at Mrs. Worth in the darkness of the truck's cab. She seemed nice. When the men had been moving off into the woods, her husband suggested that she drive Robbie to their home to wait. But when Robbie protested, Mrs. Worth took his side, saying, "We'll wait here. After all, it's his brother." She seemed to understand Robbie's feelings.

"How long have they been gone?" Robbie asked.

"About a half hour."

"They ought to be back soon."

"It won't be too long, I'm sure."

"I'm sure hungry. I'll bet Eric is too."

"We'll get you both something to eat when they all come back. It won't be long."

The voice blaring from the bullhorn—"This is the police. You are surrounded. Come out with your hands up"—was so loud that Eric was able to hear the order clearly in the small equipment room at the rear of the barn. He wanted to shout. Robbie had gotten through and found help! Now that the police were here, surely he was only minutes away from being freed, safe and unhurt.

But he stood still, hardly breathing, wondering what would happen next.

Frightening thoughts raced through his mind. Would the man named Lucas, in his anger, kill him? No, surely not. What would be the point? But he might come for him, then use him as a shield in an effort to get away into the night. Or maybe the men would tell the police to let them get away or they would kill the boy they were holding captive.

He consciously forced a better thought into his mind. Only two, maybe three, of the men even knew he was here. Maybe they would ignore him in their panic. After all, they would be frantic to escape. Or, better still, maybe they would all surrender peacefully.

Eric strained his ears to get some idea of what was happening now, some clue as to what might happen next.

At first, nobody at the table moved. Then Lucas got to his feet.

His movement seemed to break the inertia, and now all of them were scrambling. Jerry tripped on the bench trying to get up and almost fell, finally righting himself by grabbing the table. He said something that sounded like "Oh no."

Wilmer, his eyes wide, said, "Lucas, what are we going to do?"

Lucas ignored him.

"I've got a gun in the cab," Johnny said. But the truck was in the open doorway, with the cab outside, bathed in light from the barn. He did not move toward the truck.

The voice on the bullhorn spoke again: "Come out one at a time, hands over your head so we can see them."

Everyone in the barn stood still, listening.

Then Jake said in a low voice, "Outside, we'll be in the dark and we can make a break for it. If we scatter, some of us are sure to get away."

"And some of us will probably get shot," Lucas said flatly.

"But it's a chance for some of us—maybe all of us—to get away."

"I'd rather not get shot," Lucas said.

Jerry began walking toward the door, lifting his hands.

The other five watched him go.

"I always figured him to be one without a stomach for a fight," Johnny said.

"I don't see you doing nothing so tough right now," Lucas said sarcastically.

Johnny glared back at him but said nothing.

"Maybe we ought to surrender, Lucas," Wilmer said. His voice was almost a whine. "We don't have any guns, and I don't want to get hurt."

"You go ahead, Wilmer."

"Is it okay?"

"Sure."

Wilmer glanced around at the others, then walked away, raising his arms as he passed through the doorway.

Lucas turned to Jake, Johnny, and Henry. "Go on," he said. "Wilmer's right. None of us is armed, so we don't stand a chance of getting away. If we surrender peacefully, it'll go easier on us. Get going."

"What about you?" Jake said. "Aren't you coming?"

"I'll be right behind you. I just want to stash this dough."

Jake stared at Lucas for a moment. Then he nodded, turned, and started walking toward the doorway, with Henry close behind, and Johnny followed.

As soon as he was alone, Lucas quickly moved to the door of the equipment room, slid the bolt, and opened the door.

Stepping through the doorway, he spotted Eric in the shadowy light. The boy was watching him. Lucas took a pocketknife out of his jeans, opened the blade, let Eric see it, and closed the door.

He walked the couple of steps to Eric.

"I've got a knife," he said. "If you make any sound at all, I'm going to cut you—bad."

He heard the boy take a quick breath, then whisper, "Okay."

Holding the knife in his left hand, Lucas put the blade under Eric's nose. Then he quickly moved behind him, shifting the knife so it now pressed against Eric's Adam's apple. Grabbing Eric's right wrist with his right hand, Lucas wrenched Eric's hand up into the small of his back.

"I can cut your throat or break your arm, boy. Now don't be a fool." He twisted Eric's arm a little more to show he meant it.

"You don't want to hurt me, mister," Eric said through gritted teeth.

"I don't want to, no," Lucas said. "But I wouldn't lose any sleep over it if I did, either, so keep quiet."

CHAPTER 18

IT was quiet.

Eric could hear nothing but the sound of his own breathing, and the man's. The knife blade was pressing against his throat.

He wondered where the police were. Weren't they going to search the barn? Surely they'd check out the equipment room. The quiet was nerve-racking. What was happening?

Eric waited, trying not to panic, trying instead to picture how he could break free of Lucas's hold.

He couldn't do anything now—the hold was too tight, and the blade was right on his throat. But if Lucas got distracted—if he loosened his grip or moved the knife away, just a short distance, from his throat—then maybe Eric could make his move.

A quick motion upward with his left arm to knock the knife away, then a dip and a spin to the right to get his right hand free. Eric pictured it in his mind, throwing Lucas off, then throwing a punch or a kick—anything, it didn't have to be much, as long as Eric stayed away from the knife in Lucas's left hand.

Planning his escape calmed Eric. He could feel his breathing slow and his muscles relax. He was sure he would be ready if—no, he told himself, when—the moment came.

Then he heard a click, and he saw the unlocked door of the equipment room being opened. Eric could feel Lucas tense behind him, driving his arm farther up between his shoulder blades.

A narrow column of light appeared as someone slowly opened the door. Then the column widened.

A voice said, "We know you're in there, Lucas. Your brother told us you were in the barn, and this is the only place left to hide."

When Lucas said nothing, the voice continued: "Come on out. It's all over."

"I've got a boy in here with me," said Lucas, recovering. "I got a knife on him."

The officer stepped through the doorway, a flashlight in his left hand and a revolver in his right. "Let the boy go," he said. "You're in enough trouble as it is."

Eric saw something move beyond the policeman. It was another uniformed officer, just outside the door.

The officer waggled his revolver slightly. "I can

stand here as long as you can, Lucas," he said. "You might as well give it up now."

Eric couldn't help feeling a tinge of fear at the sight of the revolver—even if the officer was aiming at Lucas, not him.

"I'm coming out with the boy," said Lucas. "I'll cut him if you try to stop me." Taking the knife away from Eric's throat, he waved it at the officer.

"Don't make me shoot you."

Eric could feel Lucas sag a little. He was still waving the knife, and his grip on Eric's right wrist loosened a little.

"You won't shoot while I'm holding the boy," Lucas said, trying to sound confident.

"Try me."

Lucas jerked, surprised at the officer's response—and Eric knew his chance had come. He swung his left arm up as quickly and powerfully as he could, knocking the knife away from his throat. Then, just as he'd pictured, he dipped and spun to his right, wrenching his arm free of Lucas's grip.

Momentarily, Eric and Lucas were face-to-face. In the crazy jumping beam of the officer's flashlight, Eric could see the surprise—no, shock—on Lucas's face. Eric had the advantage now, and he meant to press it.

Still spinning to his right, he threw a punch at Lucas's head, connecting with a surprisingly loud smack on the man's temple. Lucas said, "Uh," and staggered backward a step, the knife blade glinting in the light.

Quickly, Eric jumped back, and at the same moment the officer grabbed his shoulder, pulling him through the doorway and into the main space of the barn.

Then the officer stepped back into the doorway and said calmly, "What're you going to do now, Lucas?"

Eric heard, rather than saw, the knife clunk onto the wood floor of the equipment room and Lucas say, "Darn kid, I think he gave me a black eye."

Eric didn't wait to watch the officer handcuff Lucas. As he made his way through the barn to the doors at the front, his first thought was for Robbie: Was he okay? His second thought was in answer to Lucas: Black eye, nothing—I practically broke my hand on your face.

Outside, the blackness of the night was pierced by a dozen dancing beams of light from powerful flashlights.

The police officer led Lucas toward a group of men huddled in front of the truck. Eric recognized the one named Wilmer. The red-haired man was sobbing. He figured that the other three men with them must be the ones who had arrived after he was locked away in the equipment room. They were all handcuffed to one another.

A man appeared at Eric's side. "I'm Gene Worth. Your brother is with my wife in our truck on the highway. Are you all right?"

Eric looked at the man without answering. He wasn't in uniform. He wasn't wearing a badge or carrying a gun.

Seeing Eric's questioning look, Gene Worth continued. "I'm an off-duty police officer, in case you're wondering. As luck would have it, your brother flagged me down on the highway. Now, did they rough you up any in there?"

"No," Eric said, shaking his head. "I'm okay. I hurt my hand a little hitting that guy." He nodded toward Lucas, who was tenderly touching his right eye.

"You punched him?" Officer Worth asked.

"Yeah." Eric shook his hand out. "I'm not sure I did it right—I kind of jammed my knuckles."

"Let me take a look at that." Eric held his hand out. "Can you move all your fingers?" Eric waggled them. "It's bruised, but it doesn't look like anything's broken."

"I never punched anyone before."

"It's not a good habit to fall into," said the man, smiling. "But I think it was probably necessary at the time. Now come on with me, slugger, and I'll take you to your brother. He's worried sick."

Eric grinned, happy to let Officer Worth take charge for the time being. As they walked toward the woods, a voice blared through the bullhorn: "All right, let's go, single file."

Robbie saw the flashlights twinkling in the distance through the woods, and he opened the door of the pickup truck.

"I think you'd better wait here," Mrs. Worth said.

Robbie hesitated, then said, "Okay," and closed the door. He felt a moment of panic. What if Eric was hurt—or worse? It would be because of him. His wandering away and getting lost had sent Eric into the barn. And maybe he hadn't been fast enough in reaching the highway and finding help.

Robbie wished they would hurry.

As the twinkling lights drew nearer, Mrs. Worth leaned forward and turned on the truck's headlights.

Then Robbie heard Eric's voice calling him.

Robbie glanced back at Mrs. Worth.

"It's all right, go ahead," she said.

Robbie swung open the door and tumbled out. He ran toward the sound. Then he saw Eric stepping out of the woods. He ran to him, almost jumping into his arms.

CHAPTER 19

THE caravan of five police cars followed by the Worths' pickup truck moved quickly along the dark highway. Eric was riding in the front seat of a deputy's car. Robbie was riding with the Worths. As they turned off the highway and headed for the sheriff's office, Eric spotted a fast-food shop with neon lights ablaze, and he remembered he was hungry.

When the car moved into the sheriff's parking lot and came to a halt, Eric got out and looked around. Police officers were unloading their prisoners and taking them inside. Eric watched the Worths' pickup truck drive across the lot and park at the far end.

Near the front door of the building, he saw a yellow station wagon with large red letters along the side spelling out NEWSHOUND. A short, chubby man with a bald head was getting out of the vehicle and stepping briskly toward the nearest officer. Eric heard the man say, "Hey, what's going on here?" For a moment, the man looked at Eric—the only stranger in the parking lot who wasn't handcuffed—and then he turned back to the officer. "I heard something on the radio, Billy, and . . ."

Eric walked out of hearing, away from the deputy's car, back toward the pickup, where Robbie was getting out with the Worths. He called out, "Are you okay?"

Robbie scowled. "I'm really hungry," he said.

Eric laughed. "So am I." He gestured back down the road toward the highway and said, "There's a place down there that looks open. I'll run over and get us some hamburgers."

Officer Worth came around the side of the truck. "We'll be wanting to take a statement from you," he said. "I'll ask my wife if she'd drive over there and get you some hamburgers. You and Robbie come on inside with us."

Inside the sheriff's office, Eric and Robbie sat together at a large table, waiting for their food to arrive. On the other side of the room were four officers. Eric could overhear bits of their conversation— mostly just idle chat about the weather, some charity softball game, their kids. Every now and then, they'd circle back around to the events of the evening, but they didn't seem overly concerned about it—it seemed to be all in a night's work to them.

Mrs. Worth opened the door and stepped in, placing a bag and two sodas in front of Eric and Robbie.

Then her husband walked over and said, "You boys take a minute to eat. Then the sheriff wants to talk to you."

Eric nodded, opening the bag. He handed a hamburger to Robbie, then took one for himself.

Unwrapping his food, Eric thought about the police officers chatting casually in the corner. It might be all in a night's work to them, but he was still pretty shaken up. He'd bet that Robbie was too.

"Hey," he said, "are you all right? We had kind of a rough night, huh?"

Robbie grinned. "Yeah, I'm okay. Why wouldn't I be all right?"

Eric smiled. "No reason. It's just that you had to walk through the woods all by yourself, in the dark, and I thought you might have gotten a little . . ."

"Scared?"

Eric nodded, but said nothing.

"Maybe," Robbie replied at last.

"Hey," said Eric, changing the subject. "That was some good code you worked up. It really saved the day."

Robbie tapped five times quickly on the table—"I am an eleven-year-old doofus." Then Eric slapped his hand down hard—"Not!"

The two of them started laughing.

"I'll never call you that again, I promise," said Eric, now serious. "I owe you that."

"You don't owe me anything," said Robbie, turning serious himself. "It was all my fault in the first place."

"Hey, don't worry about it. Everyone makes mistakes. Did I ever tell you about the time I lost Dad's favorite fishing pole?"

Robbie's eyes opened wide. "*You* lost Dad's fishing pole?"

"Uh, yeah. I'll tell you about it some other time. Anyway, the point is, nobody's perfect, not even me, as hard as that is to believe."

Robbie snorted, and Eric continued: "And the point is, too, that you really came through. I don't know what would've happened without you."

"Thanks," said Robbie quietly. "But, you know, I *was* scared in the woods for a little while. I thought there was a wolf or a bear in the bushes."

"What happened?"

"I was going to run away. But then I decided it would be better to stay and try to fight. Turned out it was a raccoon—no big deal."

"Hmm. But you didn't know that at first."

"No."

The two of them sat quietly for a moment.

Then Robbie asked, "Were you scared in the barn?"

"Who, me?" Eric said, then added, "I was petrified."

"Good. I was petrified too. But you stood and fought anyway, didn't you?"

"Yeah," said Eric, rubbing his knuckles. "When I had to."

Robbie looked at Eric and smiled. Eric smiled back.

When they finished eating, Eric gathered the wrappers and shoved them in the bag, then sat back. The four officers gathered around the table. "Ready, boys?" one of them said.

Eric and Robbie nodded.

"Now, tell me what happened," said the officer to Eric.

As Eric spoke, another one of the officers occasionally jotted something on a yellow pad. The man from the "Newshound" station wagon scribbled furiously in a stenographer's notebook, turning a page every few sentences. He obviously knew all the officers, and a couple of times he stopped Eric with a request that he repeat a point or a name.

"That's about all there was to it," Eric said at last. "Robbie?"

Robbie gave his own even briefer version of the events. "And here we are," he finished.

Nobody moved.

What else do they want from us? Eric wondered. Something, for sure.

Then one of the officers spoke. "What did you over-hear while you were locked in the equipment room?"

"I couldn't hear much of what they said."

"Anything—anything at all—may be useful."

"Like what?"

"Did they mention any names?"

"Names?"

"Names of the people they were working for. Names of the people who sent the three men here with the stolen cars and the truck to haul out the parts."

Eric went back over the already-blurred memory of his experience. Frankly, he hadn't been concerned with trying to catch names—he had mainly been oc-cupied with trying to save himself. Sure, he had heard names—Jake, Jerry, Lucas, Wilmer. But the officers already had those names, and the men who went with them.

"The one named Lucas," Eric said finally. "I heard him say something about 'the big shots' once, but never a name."

The officer looked at Eric in silence for a moment,

not writing down what he'd said. "Did any of them say anything about a place? If not a city, maybe a street name, a neighborhood—anything?"

"Not that I heard."

Another of the officers spoke for the first time. "Did the one who was holding a knife on you say anything about where he might be going if he got away?"

"No." Eric looked around at the police officers. He felt that he was letting them down. He should've overheard names and addresses. But if the men didn't say them, how could he have overheard them? Finally, he shrugged and said, "I'm sorry."

"Nothing to be sorry about," the officer across from him said. "Do you boys have a place to spend the night?"

Eric glanced at Robbie. Their camp was on the river. There was no way to find it in the dark.

Before Eric could answer the reporter clapped his notebook closed, got to his feet, said, "That's it," and headed for the door.

One of the officers said, "Good night, Ed," and then they all looked back at Eric.

He said, "I . . . I haven't thought about it."

One of the deputies said, "You can stay here in the jail."

"Jail!" Robbie fairly shouted.

Gene Worth took a step forward from the far wall,

where he had been standing with his wife. "We'll put them up," he said. "We've got the boys' bedroom, what with them being away at college."

It was long past midnight when Gene Worth, followed by a deputy sheriff's car with Eric and Robbie inside, turned his pickup truck onto a gravel driveway and slowly came to a halt at the edge of a carport. Leaving the lights on, he got out and walked to the car while his wife went into the house.

Eric and Robbie were getting out on the passenger's side.

Officer Worth leaned down to the driver's window and said, "C'mon in, Harvey. I'll bet Myrna could find a cup of coffee for you."

"Thanks, Gene, but I'd better be going. It's late, and tomorrow is going to come early again."

Officer Worth nodded, stepped back, and waved as the deputy backed out of the driveway. Then he turned and followed Eric and Robbie toward the house.

Inside, lights were coming on in one room after another as Mrs. Worth walked through.

Gene Worth walked Eric and Robbie through the house to a bedroom—a typical bedroom of two brothers: bunk beds, pennants and posters on the wall, a basketball trophy on the chest of drawers.

Myrna Worth, waiting for them, said, "You'll want to be calling your parents."

Eric frowned. He and Robbie could go to the campsite in the morning, load up and get the canoe out of the river, return to Gilbert for the car, and be home before dark. There was no need to worry their parents with a midnight phone call.

Before Eric could reply, Mrs. Worth said, "I think you should call them."

Officer Worth added, "Ed Robinson, with the radio station, is the correspondent for newspapers all over this area, all the way up to Springfield, Missouri. He's probably on the phone with the AP bureau in Little Rock right now. The story will be on the wires. You don't want your parents to hear it first that way."

Eric nodded. "Okay," he said. "You're right."

They went into the kitchen, and Eric sat at the table and placed a collect call to his home. His father answered, sounding sleepy, and accepted the charges. Then, suddenly wide awake and alert, he asked, "What's wrong?"

With his mother listening on an extension phone, Eric told the story as briefly as he could. When he had finished, he listened a moment, then lowered the phone, his hand over the mouthpiece, and looked at Robbie.

"They want to know if we're coming home or if we're going to finish the trip," he said.

Robbie said nothing, but the expression on his face said a lot.

Eric brought the telephone back up and said, "We're going to finish the trip. With Robbie to look out for me, nothing bad can happen."